HER HEART POUNDED WITH THE INTENSE CRAVING SHE FELT FOR HIM. . . .

She returned his passion eagerly with her own.

Drawing back slightly, Doug trailed kisses over her hair, her ear, and down her neck, his breath ragged and warm against her skin. "Let's get out of here." His voice was husky and almost desperate. "Let's go . . . somewhere."

"Yes," she breathed. She would go with him anywhere. She loved him and wanted to share all of her love with him. Her eyes flamed with passion, and she stared into his strong, handsome face.

"Yes, Doug. I want to . . . go home with you."

CANDLELIGHT ECSTASY ROMANCES™

32 SENSUOUS BURGUNDY, *Bonnie Drake*
33 DECEPTIVE LOVE, *Anne N. Reisser*
34 STOLEN HOLIDAY, *Marjorie Eatock*
35 THAT ISLAND, THAT SUMMER, *Belle Thorne*
36 A MAN'S PROTECTION, *Jayne Castle*
37 AFTER THE FIRE, *Rose Marie Ferris*
38 SUMMER STORMS, *Stephanie St. Clair*
39 WINTER WINDS, *Jackie Black*
40 CALL IT LOVE, *Ginger Chambers*
41 THE TENDER MENDING, *Lia Sanders*
42 THE ARDENT PROTECTOR, *Bonnie Drake*
43 A DREAM COME TRUE, *Elaine Raco Chase*
44 NEVER AS STRANGERS, *Suzanne Simmons*
45 RELENTLESS ADVERSARY, *Jayne Castle*
46 RESTORING LOVE, *Suzanne Sherrill*
47 DAWNING OF DESIRE, *Susan Chatfield*
48 MASQUERADE OF LOVE, *Alice Morgan*
49 ELOQUENT SILENCE, *Rachel Ryan*
50 SNOWBOUND WEEKEND, *Amii Lorin*
51 ALL'S FAIR, *Anne N. Reisser*
52 REMEMBRANCE OF LOVE, *Cathie Linz*
53 A QUESTION OF TRUST, *Dorothy Ann Bernard*
54 SANDS OF MALIBU, *Alice Morgan*
55 AFFAIR OF RISK, *Jayne Castle*
56 DOUBLE OCCUPANCY, *Elaine Raco Chase*
57 BITTER VINES, *Megan Lane*
58 WHITE WATER LOVE, *Alyssa Morgan*
59 A TREASURE WORTH SEEKING, *Rachel Ryan*
60 LOVE, YESTERDAY AND FOREVER, *Elise Randolph*
61 LOVE'S WINE, *Frances Flores*
62 TO LOVE A STRANGER, *Hayton Monteith*
63 THE METAL MISTRESS, *Barbara Cameron*
64 SWEET HEALING PASSION, *Samantha Scott*
65 HERITAGE OF THE HEART, *Nina Pykare*
66 DEVIL'S PLAYGROUND, *JoAnna Brandon*
67 IMPETUOUS SURROGATE, *Alice Morgan*
68 A NEGOTIATED SURRENDER, *Jayne Castle*
69 STRICTLY BUSINESS, *Gloria Renwick*
70 WHISPERED PROMISE, *Bonnie Drake*
71 MARRIAGE TO A STRANGER, *Dorothy Phillips*

A SPARK OF FIRE IN THE NIGHT

Elise Randolph

A CANDLELIGHT ECSTASY ROMANCE™

Published by
Dell Publishing Co., Inc.
1 Dag Hammarskjold Plaza
New York, New York 10017

ISBN: 0-440-18805-9

Printed in the United States of America
First printing—August 1982

Dear Reader:

In response to your continued enthusiasm for Candlelight Ecstasy Romances™, we are increasing the number of new titles from four to six per month.

We are delighted to present sensuous novels set in America, depicting modern American men and women as they confront the provocative problems of modern relationships.

Throughout the history of the Candlelight line, Dell has tried to maintain a high standard of excellence, to give you the finest in reading enjoyment. That is now and will remain our most ardent ambition.

The Editors
Candlelight Romances

For all the countless golfers
upon whom I had
breathless adolescent crushes.

CHAPTER ONE

Unfolding before her, the setting was like that of a huge, informal garden party. The wide-open golf course was playing host to a throng of eager spectators hoping for even the slightest chance to brush elbows with a favorite player.

The sun sat brilliantly naked against a sky of cloudless blue, with the early-afternoon air not yet too hot for comfort. Just the slightest hint of a breeze touched the fronds of the palm trees, their feathered tips lifting and swaying as the air rustled through them. In large oak trees Spanish moss draped across thick branches and brushed against the bark of lower limbs now and then.

All around, the green expanse of lush fairways presented a checkerboard design, their open areas bathed in yellow sunlight, while under the drooping canopy of palm and cypress trees spread a cool, inviting carpet of moss-green grass.

With her free hand Kat lifted her thick red shoulder-length hair off her neck, hoisting it high atop her head, to take advantage of the soft currents of air that wafted around her. The breeze against her neck, combined with the bubble of excitement she could feel in the air, sent a stimulating shiver down her spine.

She had arrived at the country club no more than an hour before, having spent the night in the parking lot of a motel in Florida's panhandle. But rising before dawn, and driving without stopping, past cattle ranches and citrus groves, she was able to make it to the central portion of the state by noon.

When she arrived at the club the parking lot was filled with cars, the pretournament activities already under way. She was lucky enough to find a spot under a large oak tree to park her van, and, so that he wouldn't get too hot, she left the windows open a few inches for Bogie, her cat.

Letting her hair fall back down over her neck, Kat hitched the heavy canvas tote bag she was carrying higher on her shoulder and, with confidence in her step, strode leisurely toward the large gray tent.

Press tents were always the same. Inevitably they all looked as though a traveling salvation show had just packed up and left town, only to be replaced by cigar-smoking, pencil-waving, floor-pacing, scoop-hungry journalists who all looked to be in dire need of some salvation.

For the hundredth time in two years Kat asked herself what she, a once sweet, naive little girl from Missouri, was now doing with a career like this. But it was too obvious for her to puzzle over for long. Golf was her life. It always had been.

While she was growing up Kat thought she was just like everybody else, that her family did just about the same things as other kids' families. It was only after she was in college that she realized how absolutely mad her family must have appeared to other people.

The standard joke in their family was that Kat had been born between the eleventh and twelfth holes. So the story went, her father waited just long enough for the new baby to be placed in a basket in the golf cart before he began harping to his wife, who had just given birth to the child: "Hurry and hit the ball, Margaret, or we'll have to let that foursome behind us play through."

In her father's opinion a house just wasn't a home if it didn't border the back nine of a golf course, and every vacation the family took had been a golfing one. Even their road maps were unlike any others she had ever seen. To heck with towns or historical markers or Stuckey's roadside restaurants; theirs were dotted with big green circles indicating—what else?—golf courses!

No one had been more disappointed than her father that Kat wasn't a good enough player to be a pro golfer. After all, the first toy he ever bought her was a plastic golf club. But she wasn't sorry. Not anymore, at least. She loved to write, and she loved golf. It was a perfect combination—except for one thing: Kat was not a man.

The rumbling din of voices in the tent ceased abruptly as Kat stepped over the threshold from bright light to shadow. It was always this way, this initial, awkward reaction to the presence of a female in the press tent. Especially to one as unique as Kat. The hard-nosed journalists never knew quite what to make of the red-haired, green-eyed beauty, dressed in snug designer jeans and T-shirt, who claimed to be one of them. But slowly, as always, the conversations resumed and things progressed as usual.

"There she is!" Roger Martin, who was seated at a table close to the entrance, yelled at her, and another, heavyset man who always smelled of cheap cigars chimed in, "Hey, Kat, we thought maybe you had decided finally to stay home and have babies."

"Yeah, Frank." She walked over to where the large,

crude man was seated and leaned over to whisper, "I'll stay home and have babies when you stay home and satisfy your wife. I'm sure the poor woman could really use it." Smiling sweetly, Kat raised her head and walked away, with Frank Willis's astonished blubbering and Roger Martin's approving hoots of laughter rending the air behind her.

After picking up her press badge from the tournament official, Kat glanced around the crowded tent at the long rows of tables and folding chairs, the typewriters, tape recorders, notepads, and cameras stationed and ready for action. The breeze found no passage among the crowd of men who were wiping the sweat from their brows, patting each other on the back, and moving back and forth from the large ice box filled with soda. Kat finally spotted Tim Barnes in one corner, deep in conversation with two other journalists. Walking over to their table, she dropped her bag onto the last empty chair.

"Kat!" Tim stood quickly and embraced her affectionately. "It's good to see you, babe." They kissed, and Tim turned to introduce her to the other two men. "Do you know John Bartlett? And this is Paul Wilford."

"Yes," she said. "John and I met at the last tournament. It's nice to meet you, Paul." Kat smiled and took the vacant chair next to Tim. Seated near the open edge of the tent, she was relieved to feel light breezes stirring around her.

"I was wondering if you were going to make it to this one." Tim popped the top of an unopened Coke can and pushed it over to her.

"Don't I always?" she asked, smiling her thanks for the drink.

"Kat follows the tour in a van," Tim explained to Paul.

"Really?" His eyebrows shot up in respect. "Do you make it to all the tournaments?"

"Just about all." She nodded, taking a long sip of the Coke. "Let's just say I've logged a few miles over the last two years."

"Tell me one tournament you've missed in the last nine months," Tim challenged.

"Well, I didn't go to the Hawaiian Open last winter. Remember?"

"That really must have hurt!" John cringed. "You missed the best one of the year. Although, I must admit, I don't remember much of the tournament." His mouth twisted sheepishly. "I'm afraid I had too many games of my own going on."

After the three men had agreed heartily on the curvaceously abundant and tanned attributes of the islands, Kat interjected, "Don't forget, I don't have the luxury of getting paid to fly to all the garden spots, like you guys. And I haven't perfected the wings for my van yet."

"You mean you write as a free-lancer?" Paul asked incredulously.

"That's right," she replied, accustomed to the quizzical reactions of people when they learned she roamed the country alone as a free-lance golf writer.

"Don't you ever get scared out there on the road alone?" John asked, and all three pairs of eyes riveted on Kat.

"No." She laughed. "I have a ferocious five-pound cat to protect me."

"Kat's cat." Tim snickered as though he were the first to make that joke.

"How about lonely?" Paul winked then, resting his arms on the table, leaning closer, and lowering his eyelids to half-mast. "All alone for all those long . . . empty . . . miles."

"If you're looking for an Academy Award, you've got my vote," Kat drawled. "But please save any armchair psychology for someone else. I've heard it all."

And she had. Over the two years she had been following the TPA—Tournament Players Association—Tour, she had been bombarded with just about every style of proposition and every bit of sage advice that men had to offer—not to mention the constant stream of worrisome mandates from her mother, to eat right and to call home if she needed money or more advice.

It was to be expected, she supposed. Basically golf lay under the institutionalized province of men. Of course, there were lots of women golfers, excellent ones, but the sport for them had never received the attention or purse that it had for the males. Kat had written articles about Nancy Lopez-Melton and Amy Alcott, but it was the Tom Watsons and the Jack Nicklauses that editors and the public really wanted to read about.

It was a conservative, elitist sport, where golf hobbyists followed up a round of eighteen holes with a game of cards and a bourbon.

The field of golf writing was no exception. It was traditionally the domain of men, and Kat was an interloper. She had found resentment, sexual harassment, and cynicism directed toward her. She had been the butt of jokes too numerous to count, and had received cold skepticism and even implacable hostility over her ability to write, on the part of both editors and male writers.

It had been a hard road, and Kat was now only just beginning to realize a modicum of success. Most editors now knew she could write at least a grammatically correct sentence, and some of her articles had even merited complimentary remarks from several other journalists.

Tim was one of those writers who respected her and treated her as an equal. At times he had been the only friendly face in a crowd, and she was forever indebted to him.

Although she had made it her usual habit not to fraternize with "the boys" after work, Tim was the exception to the rule. On quite a few occasions they had gone for pizza or drinks after tournaments, and had even taken a skiing vacation together once.

It was a purely platonic relationship, Tim fulfilling his own romantic interests elsewhere. Kat had encouraged that, and it seemed to work well for both of them. Besides which, they were from different parts of the country, so the only time they saw much of each other was at the tournaments.

The conversation among the three men had turned away from speculation as to Kat's loneliness on the road, and instead was focused on the events of the tournament, beginning that night with the tee-off dinner in the club's dining room. It was the one social event of the tournament where the press was welcome, the other nights being slotted by the players for much-needed rest or private parties. Kat was looking forward to the dinner. She rarely had the opportunity to dress up anymore, and she saw this as a pleasant diversion, with the possibility of a story lurking somewhere amidst the excitement of the gala event.

The tournament was to last four days—Thursday through Sunday. During the first two days the elimination rounds were held. Those players who, by Friday evening, didn't survive the cut would be out of the tournament. Those whose scores fell within ten strokes of the lead player would continue to play the next two days for the win.

"Well, who's your pick for the win, Tim?" Kat knew that Tim prided himself on divining the tournament champion. And, although there was no sure way of predicting a win in golf, his guess was usually correct.

"Ask me after the cut tomorrow night, and I'll be able to make a more intelligent guess. But, right now . . . well, what the hell. I'd say it's going to be between Hallberg, Strange, and Hayden."

"Hmm." Suddenly Kat regretted having asked Tim the question. She swallowed to remove the sour taste that had been activated in her mouth at the mention of one of those names. The thought that Doug Hayden might win filled her stomach with a heaving buoyancy that induced both nausea and excitement.

A commotion near another table drew the attention of the four away from their own conversation. Their talk suspended, they listened to catch wind of any news.

From vague hand-me-down comments, they learned that three or four of the players had arrived and were over near the scorekeeper's tent, like sitting ducks for fifty journalists to pounce upon.

Tim rose from his chair and grabbed a notepad. Paul and John both remained seated, declaring smugly that they weren't going to fight the crowd. They would get their interviews later. As a free-lancer having to scrounge for every tidbit she could find, Kat knew that for her there might not be a next time. She hopped up quickly and, reaching for the tape recorder in her tote bag, followed close behind Tim.

Outside the tent, she noticed that the breeze had ceased, the sun now beating relentlessly onto the slightly rolling expanse of golf course. Reprimanding herself for leaving her sunglasses in her tote bag, Kat squinted her eyes against the blinding light and tried to keep pace with the mass of reporters descending upon the poor, unsuspecting golfers.

Being on the outer fringe of the mob, she tried to force her way through the throng of men to a position where she could at least see whom she would be quoting. Several of the men, assuming she was the wife of one of the golfers, rather than a reporter, stepped aside to let her pass. It was an assumption that she did nothing to contradict, rationalizing her slight deception with an "all's-fair-in-love-and-war-and-interviewing" attitude.

Oh, damn, she groaned to herself. Standing in the front row, she was now able to see the golfers they would all be interviewing. Doug Hayden was one of them. Seeing him there, with that irritatingly lovable grin, Kat almost wished she had stayed in the tent with John and Paul.

"Well, if it isn't our all-American golf sweetheart," she murmured caustically. When the man standing next to her glared at her as if she were guilty of blasphemy, she decided she'd best keep her comments to herself.

Two of the players were small potatoes as far as a salable story went. They were very low on the money list so far this year and were not expected to improve their status with this tournament. The third man was Mark Windsor, also known as "the family man," so-called because at every tournament, no matter what the location or season, he was followed faithfully from hole to hole by his wife and five children. He was a quiet man and a little hard to get to know. Without a doubt he was likeable. But it was almost hard to find a story about Mark, because his life, like his golf game, seemed so blandly consistent.

Doug Hayden was a completely different story, and Kat both hated having to write about him and delighted in poking holes in his image. People had often asked her why she was so hard on him in her articles. What they didn't know was that if she wrote the words that really described what she thought about him, it wouldn't be fit to print.

That smug— How can he always look so damn cool? Wiping the perspiration from her own forehead, Kat cursed silently his unruffled appearance. ". . . dressed in tan slacks and green short-sleeved knit shirt," she whispered into her microphone, "that look a little too tight for golfing, if you ask me . . ." she added with distaste. The material of the shirt was stretched across his chest, the sturdy muscles of his torso and arms outlined for all to see. Irritation pressed her lips into a thin line as she found herself paying too much attention to his physique.

As much as it pained her to admit it, Doug Hayden was probably the most handsome man on the Tour. His light-brown hair was thick and carelessly groomed, blending perfectly with his carefree attitude. There were paler, almost blond strands of hair that wove through the brown, the result of his career of following the sun. His eyes were one of his best features—an intense sky-blue, surrounded by a thick fringe of lashes that were sun-bleached to match the lighter part of his hair—making him look like a healthy Swede. Tiny lines fanned out from the corner of each eye, framed by skin that was weathered a ruddy bronze.

Kat also had to admit that his thirty-three years agreed with him. While most definitely not in character, at least in appearance he had matured and mellowed since his days in Kansas City.

His mouth was now stretched into a wide, lazy smile as

he fielded questions with ease and humor from the reporters. They adored him, there was no doubt about that. He had them all wrapped around his little finger. Everyone fought to have assignments involving Doug, and editors loved to have stories about him. It never failed. Wherever the biggest crowd on the course gathered, that was where Doug would be playing. He had an easy temperament and always kept the crowd entertained with one-liners while the other, more serious players were deep in conversations with their caddies over which clubs to use on the next shots.

Doug had a certain winner's quality about him. It was nothing short of magic, the writers and sports announcers claimed. His swing was natural and effortless, he had nerves of steel, and his grip was so strong, he was known by the analysts as a "hands" player. In Kat's opinion it was an analysis that applied off the golf course as well as on.

He had moved up the ladder of success from rookie-of-the-year nine seasons ago and through the years following as one of the most popular players and one of the biggest money winners. So far this year alone he had finished in the top ten in all but three of the tournaments.

He was the sweetheart of the links to all—except Kat. To her, his presence alone was enough to give her claustrophobia. There had been a time three years ago when Kat was simply an above-average golfer on the amateur circuit in Kansas City. They met for the first time when Doug had been her partner in the Gentlemen-Ladies Pro-Am charity tournament in Springfield, Missouri. *She* had been wrapped around his little finger then, too. She was blinded by his boyish charm, his sparkling and inexhaustible wit, and his devastatingly handsome face and body. But no more. That period of her life was dead and buried, never to be resurrected.

Kat listened to the questions and answers, and kept her tape recorder running as the crowd around her laughed and relaxed under Doug's easy rapport with them. As usual he stole the show, and most of the questions were directed exclusively to him.

When there was a slight break in the questions, Kat interjected. "Could you tell us, Mr. Hayden," she began in contrast to everyone else's use of his first name. "In Atlanta last month, you seemed to be having considerable trouble with your swing. I was wondering if you have been practicing that in the interim."

Doug's face retained the open, attentive expression, but his steel-bright eyes seemed to take on a devilish glow as his attention centered on Kat. He was struck again—as he was whenever they crossed paths—with how beautiful she was. And, though he knew the diversions of his thoughts would play havoc with his golf game, he couldn't help but fantasize briefly about her soft, naked body under him.

There was a lazy glint in his sparkling eyes as his gaze swept boldly down her body, devouring, traveling almost by inches from her red hair to her sandaled feet and back up again. Despite her fair and rather sensitive skin, she had developed a decent tan for the first time in her life, and it gave her a healthy, vibrant glow. But the heat of embarrassment was rushing into her cheeks, staining them red, and she knew that every man there was aware of Doug's blatantly sexual perusal.

"As I recall from your last article, Miss Ingles, you suggested that I practiced swinging a little too much." There was only a slight pause for effect before he laughed mischievously. "But then, maybe you weren't referring to my golf game." The desired result was just as he had planned. A ripple of laughter bubbled through the crowd of male journalists. Kat's mouth tightened automatically, and her body stiffened at having been the butt of one of Doug Hayden's typically chauvinistic jokes.

"But then, maybe I read it wrong." Obviously he wasn't through with her yet, and she braced herself for the attack that was bound to come. "Sometimes"—he smiled wickedly—"it's a little hard for me to decipher the essence of some of your articles, Miss Ingles. But, perhaps it's simply because I'm not the literary type." He widened his smile to encompass the entire group. "You know what they say about athletes—all brawn, no brains."

If he had wanted to strike a low blow, which he obviously did, he couldn't have found a better way to do it than to attack her writing ability. Kat had struggled so hard to get as far as she had, and she had to hold fast continuously to keep from slipping down the treacherous rungs of the ladder. But here she was, being lambasted in a subtle way by the man she most despised—and in front of her fellow journalists. It was a vicious blow.

She curled her hands into tight fists at her side and stifled a scream of frustration. She had to maintain her composure!

Rising militantly to the attack, she tilted her head at a defiant angle and retorted, "You're probably right about that . . . the brawn vs brain syndrome. However, I wasn't aware that you took time away from your . . . swinging . . . to read my articles. I suppose I should be flattered."

Doug's twinkling blue eyes swept over the resistant planes of Kat's face, quietly questioning and appraising, while at the same time mocking her discomposure.

The exchange between the two had been reduced to a

personal battle, and the other reporters were beginning to fidget and lose interest. Sensing this, Doug deftly wrapped up the interview. "I think we'd better call this quits and get on with our golf practice now. If any of you have any further questions, I'll be glad to try and answer them after my practice round." Laughing heartily and drawing the attention of everyone in the crowd, he added as a final note, "I'm afraid Miss Ingles will have to sharpen her claws on someone else today."

With a roguish grin directed toward Kat, Doug stood calmly, waiting for her response.

That son of a— Oh, she couldn't even find a word vile enough to describe him! Well, he had humiliated her once before, three years ago, and she had not forgiven him. And, if he thought he was going to do it again, he had another think coming. She would show him. The power behind her pen could be much deadlier than the power behind his big mouth.

With an exterior show of calm that she was not feeling inside, Kat met Doug's gaze in a deadly confrontation, her eyes wavering only slightly when she noticed the triumphant flash of amusement that sprinted across the surface of his eyes. Not about to let him have the last move, she pivoted sharply on her heels and pushed her way through the crowd, away from him. But she could hear the sound of his throaty laughter trailing her, and it echoed through her mind with resounding mortification.

CHAPTER TWO

Wearily Kat pulled the keys from her tote bag and unlocked the door to her silver van. Lifting a foot that felt as burdensome as a lead weight, she climbed inside.

Unlike most standard vans, hers had been customized by adding an extra three feet to the top so that she could stand without stooping. The carpet was a medium shade of gray, a color that showed every trace of dirt, and one she would replace in a minute if she had the money.

At the back of the van was a royal-blue corduroy couch that converted into a double bed. Underneath were cabinets for storage of bedding and luggage. In front of the bed was a fold-out table for meals and writing. A small refrigerator, a sink, and a two-burner stove were built against one wall, and on the other wall was a tiny bathroom with a shower. Curtains in blue and gray covered the window behind the couch, and a long draw curtain could divide the driver's area from the living section of the van.

It wasn't the Ritz, that was for sure, but it was home, and had been for the past two years. And she had adapted to it.

After she had graduated from college Kat spent over a year working on her golf game to the exclusion of almost everything else. Her parents were well-to-do, so she didn't have to worry about a full-time job. However, she did write a couple of short stories that were published by a leading women's magazine. Not only did they give her a little extra spending money, but they also relieved her conscience somewhat. Though she wanted nothing more than to play golf, she did at times feel guilty over the fact that she didn't have a regular job, like most of her friends.

She wasn't sure when it was that she became disillusioned with her plans to become a golf pro. Was it when she realized that, though a good player, she simply wasn't good enough to make it as a pro? Or was it when she met Doug? She had never drawn a definitive conclusion, but assumed that it was probably a combination of both.

Whatever it was that made her turn to another career, she was happy with the one she had chosen. She couldn't stand the idea of working at a desk job for eight hours each day, nor could she bear the thought of deserting the two things she enjoyed most—golf and writing. She knew there might come a day when she no longer wanted to travel so much. But then, nothing in life was permanent. For the moment, she was content with things the way they were, and she had no intention of quitting the profession when she was only halfway up the ladder of success. There was still a long way to climb, and she would hang in there, grasping and pulling to make it to the top.

Setting her tote bag in one of her captain's chairs, she scooped Bogie off the driver's seat and cradled him close to her. "Hi, baby," she crooned. "How was your day? Better than mine, I hope." She sighed, setting the cat on the floor and filling a bowl full of fresh water for him.

It had been an exhausting afternoon, and the tournament hadn't even begun. If she could just stay away from Doug Hayden for the next few days, she would be all right.

That was what was so draining about today. Trying to dodge his criticism and land a few blows herself had sapped every ounce of energy in her body.

She had been in such high spirits when she arrived at noon. She was looking forward to everything about the Lakeburg Classic. It was one of the most prestigious tournaments, with one hundred and forty top golfers in the country competing. The club was to be awash in celebrities and members of the press, and Kat was sure she could get a salable story out of it.

But, after her verbal duel with Doug that afternoon, the scene no longer looked quite so much like a garden party; it was more like an ill-fated battlefield. Why did she let him get under her skin that way? Why couldn't she be more like him? No matter what she wrote about him, or how much she might insinuate or even stretch the truth about him, he never got angry. He always just smiled, crinkling his laughing blue eyes, and gave her no satisfaction in knowing that she had punctured his ego at all. That's what it was! That's what made her so furious, she could spit nails! What she did or said had no effect whatsoever on him.

Well, to hell with him, she thought, slamming a cabinet door closed after reaching for a glass from the shelf. "I'm not through with you yet, Doug Hayden," she said aloud. "I've only been testing the water up until now. From now on the attack is going to be direct and deadly. You'd better watch your step, because, like you, I too can land some crippling blows below the belt."

As she stepped from the tiny shower cubicle an hour later, Kat's fatigue had vanished. The tingling spray of the cool water had soothed her tired muscles and bruised ego, and she felt relaxed and eager for the social event ahead.

Tonight was the dinner and dance in the ballroom of the country club, and everyone who was anyone in the golf world was going to be there. Kat thought it would be a great place to make some contacts and maybe pick up some lightweight quotes.

Tim was coming by to pick her up in forty-five minutes, so she would have to hustle if she was going to have her hair dried, makeup on, and be dressed by the time he arrived.

Tim was staying at a house rented by one of the leading golf magazines for its writers. Kat had long ago given up hope that she too might be invited to stay in one of the plush hotels or houses provided by the editors. They were strictly male domiciles, and the last thing the men needed before a big tournament was an attractive woman to distract them from much-needed sleep.

At least she had this van. She was humbly grateful for the loan from her father that enabled her to buy it. Without it, there was no way she could have afforded to follow the Tour around the country.

Drying it first with a towel and then a blow dryer, Kat brushed her burnished hair back from her face, letting it fan out in full, natural waves at the sides of her face.

She was a strikingly beautiful woman, but she was known to have the temperament of a determined tiger. While making no conscious effort to attract men's lascivious thoughts, Kat always captured many an admiring gaze and scores of propositions wherever she went. But few men were willing to tackle a deeper relationship with her. She guessed it was her assertive willfulness that frightened them off. Even Tim had often teased her about being a fireball too hot for any man to handle.

Taking enough time to apply her makeup properly, Kat was barely dressed before she heard the knock on the side of the van. A loop earring grasped between her teeth, she was trying to slip her high heels onto her feet while she pulled open the door.

"Hi, Tim." The words spurted around the earring in her mouth. "Come on in. I'm just about ready."

Sucking in a deep breath, then exhaling slowly, Tim expressed his admiration without words. Dressed in a Persian-blue silk-jacquard kimono with matching pants and camisole, she looked elegant and sexy at the same time.

"You look like you could use some help there."

"Yeah!" she snapped. "I fired my personal maid, so now I have to dress myself. Are you going to stand out there in the heat all night, or are you coming in?"

Reluctantly dragging his eyes away from her well-proportioned figure, Tim climbed into the van and took a seat in one of the captain's chairs. Bogie, remembering other times such as this, jumped into Tim's lap and promptly made himself at home.

"Hey, Bogie, old buddy. I think he's missed me," Tim said, grimacing slightly as he watched Kat slip the earring through a tiny hole in her ear. "He must see me as a father figure."

"Try again, Tim." Kat laughed, picking up her evening clutch purse and placing a few things inside it. "But then, come to think of it, you are kind of like a tomcat, aren't you? Always on the prowl."

"If you mean on the prowl for good-looking broads, you're right."

"Women."

"Huh?"

"Women, Tim, not broads."

"Oh . . . yeah, sorry. Don't forget your press badge." Tim changed the subject, but he knew that without it, Kat would be bounced out so quickly, she wouldn't know what had hit her.

"Right. Thanks. It was hard enough talking my way into getting a ticket in the first place." Fishing through her tote bag on the other chair, she pulled the badge from the bottom and dropped it into her purse.

"Kat, there's something I want to talk to you about." Tim shifted uneasily in his chair, disturbing Bogie out of a sound sleep. The cat bounded from his lap and crawled up into the driver's seat. "Just tell me to shut up, if you want, but—"

"Why do I feel a lecture coming on? Listen"—she sighed—"if it's about my behavior during the interview this afternoon, you're wasting your time." She had noticed the distasteful look on Tim's face that afternoon when she pushed her way out of the crowd.

"Look, Kat. I don't know what it is you have against Doug Hayden, but I do know that you're hurting your somewhat skittish reputation with the guys in the press tent."

Nibbling at her full lower lip, Kat listened without comment.

"First of all, everyone else likes him, and it really irks them that you harass him constantly. Second of all, they're beginning to think you don't look at things very objectively. That little conversation this afternoon was strictly personal. I—I just hate to see you lose your professional credibility when you've worked so hard to attain it.

If you've got something personal against Hayden, that's your business. But don't make it public, because you'll only be cutting your own throat."

Sighing heavily, Kat stared at the battleship-gray carpeting she detested so much. Tim was right. She could destroy her standing that way. She would simply have to be more discreet from now on. No more public verbal attacks against the man. She would save them instead for her articles.

"You're right as usual, Tim, and thanks for being a friend." She smiled. "I can't even count the times you've saved my neck. If it weren't for you, I'd be back in Kansas City frying drumsticks in a take-out chicken stand or something."

"Oh, heavens, Kat!" Tim laughed. "I don't think you'll ever be in straits that dire . . . unless, of course, you don't leave everyone's golf hero alone."

"Hmm," she murmured, rubbing Bogie absently behind the ear. "Well, I guess we'd better go." She not only wanted to get to the party, she also wanted to drop the conversation about Doug. "See you later, Bogie. You hold down the fort while I'm gone."

After the van was locked Kat and Tim headed leisurely up the sweeping drive of the country club to the wide entrance.

The evening was warm, but a soft, billowing breeze had picked up again, gently stirring the balmy fragrances of the tropical region. The soothing breath of night seemed to exhale luminous clouds of stars, so dense they were like motes of dust suspended in a single shaft of light. Hibiscus and bird-of-paradise filled the beds along the drive, and the delicate scent of jasmine wafted through the summer night air. To the east, just the outline of a new moon could be seen.

As they stepped over the threshold of the club's entrance, Kat's eyes widened automatically at the more earthly, but equally magnificent, glittering spectacle before them.

The walls of the foyer were covered in mauve silk. Ornamented crystal chandeliers hung from the ceiling at each end of the sumptuous lobby. The floor was marble, a pale-pink stone that resounded with the shuffling and clacking of three hundred pairs of shoes.

Beyond the foyer Kat could see through the wide doorway into the huge ballroom. Tables, covered with pale peach linen cloths, lined each wall, and a small, perfect tropicana rose was set at the head of each place setting.

Moving slowly through the crowd, Kat had to make a conscious effort to keep her mouth from gaping. Never before had she attended an event so lavish. Never before had she seen men and women dressed as elegantly as they were there.

For a minute she did a double take, thinking she must surely be at the wrong party. These weren't the same men who always wore colorful cotton slacks, and knit shirts with little alligators on the left side of the chest! These weren't the wives who followed their husbands, wearing Bermuda shorts or A-line golf skirts! The transformation was incredible.

What Kat didn't notice were the admiring stares she was receiving from every corner of the room. Very few people failed to notice the striking red-haired woman moving through the crowd with casual ease. And more than once, a knowing wife slyly had to direct her husband's attention elsewhere.

Waiters carrying trays of champagne wove through the crowd, and Tim reached for two glasses for himself and Kat. She sipped at the bubbling liquid, relishing the tingling sensation as it slid smoothly down her throat. Her earlier tensions of the day were completely forgotten, and as she drained her glass the thought of Doug Hayden was the farthest one from her mind.

Greeting the people they already knew and boldly introducing themselves to others, she and Tim threaded their way through the foyer and into the ballroom.

A long table was set in the middle of the room, containing canapés of every type, including creamed oysters, lobster spread, rolled asparagus, bread sticks, and assorted cheeses. In the center was a large sculpture of a golfer with club poised high over his shoulder, that brief moment before the club swings through to strike the ball, frozen in blue ice.

Tim was reaching for more glasses of champagne when Kat overheard the two women next to her chattering loudly. "He's gorgeous," one of them crooned. The other obviously agreed and then made a suggestive remark that Kat could not decipher. As the two women were twittering over the observation, Kat followed the direction of their appraising stares.

Across the room, she saw that Doug Hayden was the object of their gaping admiration. Curling her lips sardonically, she noticed that he was framed by a group of men and women obviously mesmerized by whatever he was saying. One gorgeous brunette in the group clung to his arm possessively, her breasts swaying precariously in the low-cut gown she wore. Kat couldn't control the sudden sharp pang of jealousy that stabbed at her.

While all the other men in the room seemed to blend

into a neutral tangle of tuxedos, none more discernible than the rest, Doug, in a contrast as vivid as that of the moon to the stars, drew her attention until everyone in the huge room paled to insignificance.

He was tall and handsome, the power beneath his lean frame always evident. She couldn't control her eyes as they were drawn to the outline of his hard thighs revealed beneath his trousers. Traveling up the length of his frame, Kat's gaze stopped at his neck. For a brief moment she had the almost unbearable desire to reach out and stroke the strong column of his tanned throat, then wind her fingers through the shafts of his thick brown hair. She felt a familiar quickening of her pulse as she watched him absently stroke the stem of his champagne glass, then lift it to his lips, drawing the clear liquid into his mouth and down his throat.

For a moment time stood still, and Kat's mind was free to wander to memories of long ago, to the feel of Doug, the desire for him. But when his piercing gaze lifted over the crowd and locked with hers, impaling her with its scorching intensity, the warm memories of what almost was were destroyed by the cold reality of what actually had been.

With a quick pivot of her head, Kat tore the vision of him from her line of sight. Her eyes shifted to Tim, who was standing beside her with the drinks and who had obviously seen Kat staring wantonly at Doug. Tim's eyes bore into her, trying to decode the message under the surface of her expression.

She felt the heat of embarrassment flooding into her cheeks, and her eyes darted about in agitation.

"Well, do I get the drink, or are you going to stand there and gawk at me all night?"

Tim slipped the glass into her hand without comment, but a perceptive smile played at the corners of his mouth.

She was rescued from more of his scrutiny when some old acquaintances walked over to them and started up a conversation.

It was several minutes later before Kat's eyes drifted involuntarily toward that spot where Doug had been standing. He was no longer there, and her pulse decelerated, leaving her with a keen sense of both disappointment and relief.

After about an hour the party began drifting toward the tables lining the walls. Kat was thankful that she had not yet been forced to speak to Doug. She most definitely did not want a repeat of the afternoon's annoying meeting. Besides, a story of his party manners was not exactly what she was looking for. She had spoken with several of the top golfers while she and Tim mingled, and she had been promised two private interviews before the tournament was over.

If tonight was any indication, she could see why more corporate and financial deals were made over three-martini lunches than in boardrooms. Normally it was a great struggle to find golfers who would consent to an interview with her. But tonight, with the flow of alcohol running thick through everyone's blood, it had been a cinch.

Seated at a table with two golfers and their wives, a well-known television sports announcer, and a professional tennis player who was also an avid golf fan, Kat again relaxed and enjoyed herself immensely.

The dinner of a consommé, Duckling Rouennaise, Potatoes Lorette, and Tomatoes Provençale was a delicious change from her usual fare of hot dogs or cheese sandwiches. The champagne continued to flow from the bottle to the glass to the throat. Conversations were light and friendly, and the blending of voices from around the room filled Kat with a warm sense of belonging. All in all it was turning into a delightful evening.

While dessert was being served several members of the golf association stepped up to the podium at the front of the room to make a few remarks. Their speeches were very brief, blessedly so, but what followed made Kat wish they had lasted much longer.

When the president of the association asked Doug Hayden to come up to the front and make a few remarks on behalf of all the golfers participating in the tournament, Kat felt as if a sickness were spreading through her.

Watching him step up to the podium, full of ease and self-assurance, Kat seethed inside. Despite her momentary lapse earlier in the evening, she still harbored unbending hostility toward Doug. How could everyone else be so blind to his faults? What could they possibly see in him that was so wonderful? It was an easy question to answer, she grudgingly admitted. She too had once thought the sun rose and set in him.

As she sensed the crowd being hypnotized by his silver tongue and dry wit, a grim expression covered her face, and her mouth was compressed into a tight, hard line.

Everyone in the huge room was roaring with laughter and approval over his jokes, and only Tim was aware that Kat's face held no trace of amusement.

When Doug finished and moved away from the podium to sit down, the enthusiastic applause thundered in Kat's ears, invoking a raging storm of angry emotions. Only after the applause had died down and the conversations resumed did she regain some of her earlier enjoyment of the evening.

After the dessert plates were removed and the champagne glasses were refilled, the strains of music from the band shifted to softer, swaying sounds. Before long the dance floor was inundated with couples gliding to the music.

Tim and Kat were no exception. Tim was a good dancer, and they both moved together easily around the floor. The volume of champagne Kat had consumed had taken its toll, and inside she felt a warmth and softness that she hadn't felt in a long time.

Instinctively and involuntarily her body suddenly stiffened, and a shudder of apprehension shook her as she saw Doug Hayden heading straight for her. His eyes claimed her even before he tapped Tim's shoulder to cut in.

As Tim graciously stepped aside, Kat was whisked into Doug's arms before she could refuse, but her mouth flared open in mute indignation. His arms held her more firmly than Tim's had, sensing perhaps that she would flee if given half a chance. Staring straight over his shoulder, so as to avoid eye contact, she could nevertheless feel the burning spike of his gaze as it moved over her hair, her face, her body.

She held herself stiffly, saying nothing, holding her breath until the song was over and he would go away. Please don't say anything. Just have your dance and then leave, she thought.

"You look delectable tonight, Katherine," he murmured next to her ear. "As usual." As Doug swung her in his arms Kat was pulled even closer to his body, and she could feel an unwanted heat spreading across her body where it touched his.

"The name is Kat, if you don't mind," she flared, angry

with him for putting thoughts in her mind that she would just as soon have kept buried.

"Oh, but when I think of you . . . which is often . . . I always think of you as you were before. As Katherine. It sounds so much more soft and . . . willing."

How long was this damn song going to last! She tried desperately to think of some cutting remark that would send him away, but none came to mind. She couldn't think straight at all with his warm breath fanning her cheek and his large hand splayed across her back, burning through the thin silk of her kimono and into her skin.

"Loosen up, Katherine." His mouth nuzzled her ear. "You're going to tire yourself out fighting me this way. And then you won't have enough energy to throw your literary daggers at me." His low chuckle brought her up even more stiffly in his arms.

Her face accidentally touched his hair, and she noticed that it smelled fresh like the sun and the wind. Even dressed as elegantly as he was, mingling in a formal setting like this, he seemed more a part of the outdoors: as untamed as the wind in the pristine calm of day and as bold as a spark of fire in the purity of night.

Was he at the dance alone? Surely not. Doug Hayden was never without a female companion. But, if he was . . . maybe he would come back with her to her van and—God, what was she thinking!

Irritably putting a halt to the unwanted diversions of her mind, she retorted, "If you're expecting some lavish compliment from me on your speech, you're going to be waiting a long time."

"You were listening?" he taunted. "I could have sworn by your vacant expression that you were miles away

. . . or maybe just remembering another time, another place."

"What is it you want from me, Doug?" she asked, a headache of frustration beginning to throb violently at her temples.

"I want us to be friends." Keeping his arms tight around her waist, he pulled his head back to look at her. His blue eyes were muted and soft under the dim lights, but his gaze danced impishly across her face, pausing to rest on her lips, and a boyish grin played across his mouth.

"We tried that once," she flared, trying to tear herself from his strong grip. "As I recall, that worked about as well as a balloon with a hole in it. It deflated quite rapidly . . . or perhaps you've forgotten."

Pulling her back into the firm fold of his arms, he whispered, "I remember how good it was between us."

"It was never good," she snarled, "because there was never anything between us."

"Ah, but how close we came to making our dreams a reality," he crooned, with obvious delight over her discomfiture.

"Dreams!" she huffed, frantically working, to no avail, at pushing him away. "Your dreams maybe, but they were nothing short of nightmares to me. Now, if you'll excuse me, the song is finished and I have a date to return to."

He reluctantly loosened his hold on her body. "You mean him?" She followed the path of Doug's eyes to where Tim was standing at the bar, his complete attention absorbed by the petite blonde standing next to him.

Sighing in frustration, Kat twirled back toward Doug and barked, "Good night, Mr. Hayden. You'd probably better get plenty of rest tonight. I'm sure you'll need it for tomorrow . . . if not for your comedy-on-the-course routine, then at least for your game." Without another glance in his direction, she sauntered back to her table, unaware of the frown that knitted Doug's brows as her hips tantalized him with their seductive swaying.

CHAPTER THREE

Time was starting to slip into the early hours of morning. The sounds of the diminishing night drifted through the open window of the van, breathing their lullaby over Kat's sleeping form. Occasionally she shifted in the bed, finding comfort first on her back, then on her side, and finally on her stomach.

The crickets' continuous chirping reverberated in the air, and Bogie curled contentedly at the foot of the bed and slept, undisturbed by the sounds of nature. Only when the sound of whistling—a human eccentricity—overshadowed all others did Bogie raise his head and begin pacing back and forth across the covers.

Kat stirred and slowly opened her eyes at the cat's restlessness. Starting to push the little pest off the bed, she heard a loud tapping at the door. She wasn't expecting any visitors. It must be the middle of the night!

The tapping was insistent, so she pushed herself slowly from the bed and slipped on a pair of jean shorts. She had worn a long white T-shirt to bed, so at least with the shorts she appeared somewhat presentable.

She flicked the curtain aside over the sink and groaned aloud at the sight before her. What in the hell was he doing here?

She shoved open the metal door with an impatient huff and glared sleepily at the man outside.

Wearing his golf hat backward and grinning sheepishly, Doug waved a half-empty bottle of champagne high in the air, then, showing two glasses in his other hand, held the bottle out to her in invitation.

"What do you think you're doing?" Kat's hands were on her waist, and her look was filled with disdain. "Do you know what time it is?" she chided.

"No, do you?" He smiled.

He was no longer wearing the jacket to his tuxedo, and his white shirt was open at the neck and his sleeves were rolled up on his forearms. Her eyes were drawn automatically to the length of his legs beneath the well-fitted trousers. His powerful thighs seemed to taunt her with memories of their strength as they had pressed against her.

"You're drunk!" Kat, suddenly feeling weak, leaned against the frame of the door, thinking by all rights that she should slam it in his face.

He glanced around innocently, as if trying to determine who would dare have the audacity to awaken this fair creature while in a state of drunkenness.

"What do you want, Doug?" She sighed in exasperation.

"I told you earlier. I want us to be friends." He was weaving slightly as he moved closer to the door.

"And I told you we tried that." She stood straight in the opening, blocking the entrance in case he got any ideas of entering.

"We never tried to be . . . friends, Katherine." His voice suddenly sobered with a seriousness that brought out the husky quality she remembered so well.

He was right. They hadn't tried to be friends. Their

attraction for each other had been strictly physical, and after that one humiliating night three years ago, she had never wanted to see his face again, much less become friends.

What could make her want to try now? For the past two years she had raked Doug over the coals in more than a few articles. And she had enjoyed it immensely. It relieved her of the defeat she had suffered at his hands three years ago. It purged her of any guilt she might have felt from the situation, and it exorcised the demon Doug Hayden, who persistently haunted and plagued her deepest thoughts.

Why should she want to alter the status quo at this point? In what way could it possibly benefit her? Ah, but then maybe he was looking for a way to benefit himself. Perhaps the things she said about him in print really did affect him more than she thought. Perhaps by making her his friend, this was his way of getting her off his back. Well—she smiled inwardly—this could be very interesting after all. She might even find a story in it somewhere. Or, if not a story, at least some new insight into the Doug Hayden mystique. Sure, why not? This might just turn out to be the break she'd been looking for.

Stepping away from the door, she gestured with her hand for him to enter. She caught the look of surprise in his eyes when he realized she was going to let him come in without further arguments. Not wanting him to get suspicious of her motives, she reminded herself not to appear too eager to pursue this friendship.

Without a hint of his earlier inebriation, Doug stepped up and inside the van. At first he stooped, thinking the height would not accommodate his six feet three inches.

But when he realized there was plenty of room, he straightened and glanced around at Kat's home.

"Ah, so this is where the fair witch comes each night to spin her long-winded tales of scandalous golf scores, of harrowing drives and gruesome putts, of tragic lies in sand traps, and of players' tarnished reputations."

"It's a good thing you're a golfer and not a writer." Kat smirked as she leaned against the counter.

"Oh, really?" He sounded surprised. "You think I went a little overboard with the adjectives?"

"I think you went overboard with whatever you've been drinking tonight."

Doug shrugged his shoulders and smiled before moving to the back of the van and sitting on the bed. Testing it for its comfort, he finally decided it would do quite nicely. He leaned back with his head on the pillow and closed his eyes.

Kat was outraged at his presumptuous attitude. "When you said you wanted to make friends, I didn't realize you were planning to move in." Her voice had a definite snarl to it, and he opened one eye to peer at her.

"Just resting my eyes for a minute, love. I've got a big day ahead of me tomorrow."

With angry swiftness she moved to the side of the bed, tugging at his leg to remove him from the mattress. "You can just take your rest and your you-know-what elsewhere, Mr. Hayden. Now, would you please—"

He had risen halfway up, with his weight resting on his elbows. Before she could complete her command for him to remove himself from her bed, he reached out an arm and, grasping her waist, pulled her down on top of him. He was holding her fast, and the strength of her anger as she fought him was almost too much for him to control.

But rolling over on top of her, he pinned her arms above her head and her body down with the weight of his.

"Damn you, Doug! Get off of me!" Kat was sputtering with helpless rage, intensified by the smile of satisfaction on Doug's face.

"I've wanted to feel you under me like this for a long time, Katherine." His low voice washed over her, filling her with a mixture of deep-seated anger and restless craving. The desire was stronger, but it was also the more dangerous emotion, and she fought to keep it in check.

"Doug, I swear if you don't get off me this minute, I'll scream." Her eyes darkened with determination, and she saw by the flicker in his expression that she had convinced him she would do it.

She felt his hands relaxing one minute, then tightening the next. "All right, Katherine. I'll let go, but"—he pressed her down into the bed with his weight, and his right hand tunneled under the mass of her hair—"promise me that you won't get off the bed while we talk." He waited for her to reply, then gritted his teeth. "Promise me."

"Okay." She sighed, relieved that he was going to let her go. "I promise. Now, will you get off of me?"

Loosening his grip, Doug rolled to the side, and Kat sat up quickly on the bed, pulling her knees up and wrapping her arms protectively around her shins.

Wanting to be angry with him, but not sure what to say, she grabbed at the most logical way to hurt him. "Why aren't you home in bed? I know you think you're God's gift to the game of golf, but even *you* need sleep to see the ball."

She wanted to goad him, wanted to make him angry so he'd leave. But he lay there with his hands behind his head and that infuriating grin on his face. "God's gift to women, maybe, but I'm not so sure I can claim the other title."

"Oh, you are so smug, Doug Hayden."

"Hey, this isn't the way to make friends." He sat up on the bed and reached out to shake her hand. "Let's call a truce. No more name-calling, okay?"

Why should I? she wondered. But then she had decided to play along, hoping to get a story out of this. So, what could it hurt? "Okay, Doug. Truce." She met his hand in a clasp, feeling the strong fingers wrap around her smaller ones. But the friendship deteriorated at that point, for all it took was the touch of his palm against hers to stir her pulse into a state of alertness.

She pulled her hand back abruptly, not wanting to feel that automatic quickening in the core of her body. Not with Doug, anyway. There were too many other men with whom she could satisfy her desires if she wanted to. Though she wasn't in the habit of inviting men home with her, she knew that all she had to do was say the word, and she would have her pick of suitable companions for the night. She was not so desperate that she had to stoop to the level of Doug Hayden to provide fulfillment.

"All right, let's get on with it," she barked. "I've got to get some sleep."

"Get on with it?" he asked with a seductive slur. "Is that another way of saying 'get it on'?"

"Very funny." She sniffed derisively at his attempt at humor. "Look, are you satisfied that we're friends now? Will you please go home and get some sleep?"

"No." He jumped off the bed and reached for the champagne and glasses on the counter. Returning to the bed, he uncorked the bottle with ease and poured the bubbling liquid into the glasses. "First a toast." He handed her a glass and held his in the air. "To us . . . friends!"

He tipped his glass slightly in salute, then lowered it to his lips and drank, his azure-tinted eyes watching her over the rim, impaling her with their unflinching directness. Kat's breath caught in her throat, and an electrical shock coursed through her body. It took all her effort to calm her jittery nerves enough to drink. Watching him warily, she took a sip and found herself enjoying the taste more than she thought she would at that hour.

Bogie, who had been hiding under a captain's chair in front until he was sure this stranger meant no harm, now sauntered slowly down the length of the van and leaped onto the bed beside them.

"Hey, who is this?" Doug reached out to scratch the gray cat behind its ears.

"That's . . . Bogie." She relinquished the information with a slight hesitation. She wasn't sure she wanted Doug to know much of anything about her, her life, or her belongings.

"After the actor?" he inquired.

"No, my golf game." She took too large a swallow of champagne and almost choked.

"Now, I know that's not true." His hand reached out to rub and pat Kat's back gently. "You were a good golfer."

"Hmm." She stared at the liquid in her glass, wanting more than anything for him to remove his hand from her body. "But not good enough."

"Not everyone can be a professional golfer, Katherine." His voice was soft and gentle and, though she knew this charade at being friends was nothing more than an act, she found herself revealing more of herself to Doug than she wanted.

"Yeah, well tell my father that." It was only rarely that she felt guilty over dashing her father's hopes for her. He had never acted disappointed in her, but she knew he was. She could feel it deep inside. At one time she had wanted to blame Doug for her father's and her own lost hopes, but she no longer did. She knew that her inability to be a great golfer was no one's fault but her own.

"Some people are great at some things, and some are great at others." Doug's eyes were moving compassionately across the surface of Kat's face. "You're a writer, and, as you said, I'm definitely not."

"Are you going to tell me I'm a great writer?" She had meant that to sound sarcastic, but strangely enough it came out as a request.

Their eyes locked in a long moment of honest, silent communication, then Doug finally shrugged. "Well, it's kind of hard for me to be objective on that point. After all, ninety percent of your articles have been at my expense."

"You mean you actually do read them?" She smirked, feeling as if she had won a point in her favor.

"Sure I do," he answered truthfully. "I read everything that's written about me."

"You love wallowing in your own glory, is that it?" Her voice had turned cold and bitter, and the newfound friendship had lost its fresh quality.

"That's right, Katherine. I do." His voice too had a sharp edge to it. "Look, I'm at the peak of my career. Why shouldn't I relish what I've achieved? Why shouldn't I enjoy the role while it lasts? I'm not foolish enough to believe it will last forever, so for now I'm going to make the most of it. How can you find fault with that?"

She couldn't find fault with it. But, if she chewed on it a bit, she was sure she could twist it enough to where she would have a juicy quote that would make Doug Hayden look like a pompous ass. This story was going to take some serious thought, but she was sure she would have something she could be proud of.

"Katherine." Doug's voice interrupted her sadistic train of thought, and she answered with impatience.

"The name is Kat!" She hadn't been called Katherine for two or three years, and it irritated her for Doug to use her full name as if he owned it.

"I'll never be able to call you Kat," he said. "It sounds too impersonal."

"Fine, then don't call me anything," she barked. "You've heard the saying . . . don't call me, I'll call you."

"Katherine." He acted as if she hadn't spoken at all. "I know you hated me for what happened in Kansas City, but I would have thought by now that you would have changed or grown up or forgiven or— Hell, I don't know, but something," he half growled.

At his mention of Kansas City and their brief interlude when Kat was twenty-three, she tried to jump from the bed, as if by moving away from him, she could move away from the remembrance of it all. But, before she could escape, he grasped her arm and held it firmly.

"You promised you'd stay on the bed," he reminded her.

Sinking back onto the rumpled covers, she sighed, a sense of defeat washing over her. She had wanted this conversation, this silly little attempt at friendship, to stay on an impersonal level, strictly superficial, but his reference to that moment so long ago broke through the surface layers into the very core of her being.

Maybe it had been her overly protected upbringing. Her parents had guarded her life and thoughts so carefully that she had tasted very little of the world's tempting fruits of pleasure. And, at twenty-three, she had not understood deceit in any form. Even the justifiable kind. She had believed, naively, in the fairy-tale kind of love: the boy-meets-girl-fall-in-love-get-married-live-happily-ever-after type. That was the way it would be for her, and that was the way it was for other people, too. After all, she had seen it in her own parents. She had watched their love for each other grow throughout the years and had assumed that all relationships were the same.

It had been the wrong time in her life to meet a man like Doug. She was full of her own blossoming sexuality and completely blinded by a rose-colored view of life. Doug was thirty, a rising star on the TPA Tour, sure of himself, arrogant and cocky, full of his own hopes and aspirations. He was the boast of Kansas City, the new breed of golfer for the Tour. Though she had heard of him often enough and had even watched him play once, she had never met him until the Springfield tournament.

There, when Kat had been teamed with him, she had learned firsthand why he was so popular. First of all he was an excellent golfer, never getting ruffled like some players when he sliced his ball instead of hooking it. He had the uncanny ability to toss a joke out to the gallery watching him only seconds before he was to shoot. Then, moving up to the ball, his mind became all concentration, every nerve ending activated to that one purpose—hitting the ball.

It had been very easy for her, at such an impressionable and almost pathetically naive stage in her life, to fall in love with him. At every turn he flattered her, stroked her ego with positive comments, encouraged her with his winning smiles. Even more, when she graced him with one of her smiles, he acted as if the gods had placed the sun in his hands as a gift. He was chivalrous, funny, and probably the most handsome man she had ever known. He was perfect.

When the tournament was over and it was time to return to Kansas City, she felt as if her world would collapse. She was hopelessly in love with him and was afraid she'd never see him again. Even though they lived in the same city, he traveled nine or ten months out of the year, and she had no reason to believe that she would meet up with him again.

During the tournament he never treated her with anything but the utmost respect, and she wished wholeheartedly that, just once before they went home, he would not be so respectful.

After loading her golf bag and suitcase into the car in which she had ridden to Springfield, she walked over to Doug's car to say good-bye.

As she stood there, rambling on about anything but what she was really feeling, her sea-green eyes, so full of love, were met by his steady sky-blue ones. For a fleeting moment she saw a peculiar sadness sweep across the surface of his face, gone as quickly as it had appeared.

Cupping his hand against her flushed cheek, he smiled and looked at her for the first time in a less than respectful way, which filled Katherine with the fiery intimation of what all her girl friends had been talking about for years.

"May I call you in a few days?"

Not trusting her voice, she could only nod.

"I will, then."

It was a promise he kept, though it seemed more like an eternity to Katherine than only a few days.

When he did call he asked her to meet him at a party some golfer friends were having. Katherine knew several of the people there, so she felt at ease and comfortable around those who had the same interests she did.

Doug was there when she arrived, and for several blissful hours she felt a joy she had never experienced before. He kept his arm around her, refilling her drink, and her plate with food, devoting all of his attention to her and her every need. They smiled and they touched and they danced, and Katherine noticed more than one eyebrow raised at their budding relationship. But, since half of those dubious glances came from the women at the party, Katherine knew that their looks disguised the envy they were really feeling.

It was around midnight when she and Doug walked out of the apartment and strolled together through the park across the street. It was a perfect summer night in Kansas City, and Katherine knew that in that moment she would live forever, happy and in love, her fairy-tale dream life come true. It was easy to picture the two of them married and playing professional golf together. Their relationship was simply too perfect to be anything other than everlasting.

Katherine leaned against a large elm tree and, on each side of her head, Doug rested his palms against the bark of the tree.

"Katherine, I think I should tell you something. You probably already know, but in case you don't—"

She knew he was referring to his travel. He would be on the road so much, it would be difficult to maintain a solid relationship. And, too, if she went professional, she would be traveling constantly. But she knew they could make it work. She had never felt more strongly about anything in her life.

Sliding her arms up his chest and around his neck, she smiled sweetly, interrupting his confession. "I don't care. It doesn't matter, as long as we make the most of the time we have together."

In the half-light of the moon, Katherine thought she saw again that fleeting sadness on his face, but she dismissed its importance, knowing that he was still worried about the travel.

With her face upturned to his, he slowly leaned toward her, brushing slightly parted lips across hers, softly and gently until he felt her angling toward him. When her body arched ever so slightly against his, his mouth opened over hers, his tongue moving in teasing circles on her lips, prodding and caressing. When his arms circled her and pulled her tightly against his hard frame, her lips parted, and his tongue took full control of her mouth, sending shock waves reverberating through her entire body. Her skin was on fire. Everywhere he touched her, electrical jolts shot through her nerves.

His hand slipped beneath the thin material of her blouse and kneaded the flesh with an urgency that she met, touch for touch. His fingers moved beneath her bra and closed around one throbbing breast, stiffening even more its already aroused nipple. Her own hands were roaming underneath his shirt, across his back and chest, exploring.

When his hand glided under the waistband of her skirt, she thought her body would explode with the intense heat of her yearning.

She was aware constantly of every spot on his body that touched hers, and yet it all seemed to blend into a single, complete harmony of desire. Pressed tightly against the lower half of his body, she felt his hardened need for her, and she knew that, on this night, she would become his woman.

Her heart pounded with the intense craving she felt for him, and she eagerly returned his passion with her own.

Drawing back slightly, Doug trailed kisses over her hair, her ear, and down her neck, his breath ragged and warm against her skin. "Let's get out of here." His voice was husky and almost desperate. "Let's go . . . somewhere."

"Yes," she breathed. She would go with him anywhere. She loved him and she wanted to share all of her love with him. Her eyes flamed with passion, and she stared into his strong, handsome face. "Yes, Doug. I want to . . . go home with you."

He turned his head quickly, and she saw the tightening of his cheek muscle. His eyes and his jaw clenched hard for one swift second before he turned back to smile down at her. Wrapping his arm around her shoulder, he buried his face in her hair. It was a still moment between them when neither of them moved or breathed. They walked back to the party, where she had left her purse. Their steps were now quick, as if neither wanted to lengthen the time before they were again in each other's arms. There was a sense of urgency in their looks and a passionate clutching in their arms locked around each other's waists.

When they entered the harshly lighted apartment, Katherine suddenly felt as if she were in the center of a film in slow motion. At first she thought it was because they had been in the dark and had come into the light,or because they had been so intensely involved with each other and with their frenzied need to touch and kiss, and then, back at the party, everything seemed to scream reality at them.

The first thing she noticed was the tightening of Doug's arm around her, a grasp that had nothing to do with passion. She turned to stare at his now alert, taut expression and was shocked by the cold, hard profile she saw on him.

There were stares of sympathy around them, and there were the smug expressions of those who seemed to be saying "I could have told you this would happen."

Out of the sea of apprehensive faces a woman stepped forward. Katherine didn't hear many of the words she was screaming, but she heard her tone of voice and saw the raging bitterness in her eyes. She was accusing them of—what! Infidelity! That's ridiculous. Neither of them was married. How could they be . . .

When it finally soaked in that this raving woman was Doug's wife, Katherine had been reduced to stinging tears of frustration and humiliation.

She stared at Doug, willing him to deny it, to tell her that this was not his wife, that he belonged to no one else. She remembered looking at his hand and seeing no ring. But his eyes told her all she needed to know. He *was* married. This *was* his wife.

Katherine had meant nothing more to him than a night of light entertainment, as if he were out for an evening with the boys. Trite, insignificant fun! And he had humiliated her in front of all their friends, the golfers she had to play with and against, the people she had to see time and time again, with their all-knowing, sanctimonious stares.

She would never forget the disgrace of that night, the shame he put her through. If there was one moment in her life when she could say "That was when I lost my innocence," it was that night. It did not happen in the way she had planned, but she lost it all the same. Never again would she have blind trust in anyone. Never again would she believe in the fairy-tale bliss of love. And she would never . . . ever . . . forgive Doug Hayden for the dream he destroyed in her.

Time, as the cliché foretold, healed many of the wounds. She was grateful, in a way, that she had lost most of her naiveté. She had learned a great deal that night—about love and trust and deceit.

At first she blamed Doug for ruining her golfing career. It was after that one episode that her game slowly began to fall apart. She didn't seem to have the concentration, the power, the confidence, that she had had before. And she was sure that it was Doug's fault. Of course, now she knew that her game had nothing to do with anyone but herself, and it would be childish still to blame him for her own inadequacies. No, she had forgiven him that.

Also, she had learned later of his loveless marriage. He married when he was twenty-four years old and on top of the amateur golf circuit. His wife's father was extremely wealthy and wanted nothing more than a son-in-law who could play professional golf. If he would simply marry the man's daughter, Doug was assured that he would find it much easier financially to break into the pro tour. Doug liked Melissa, his wife, and he believed that love would come in time. He knew that she desired him. Their physical relationship couldn't have been better. What he didn't realize, until after they were married, was that Melissa desired nearly every man she came into contact with, and usually satisfied those desires.

Doug tried to make the marriage work, tried to find something about her to love, but it eventually became obvious that she didn't care if he loved her or not. At the same time, she wasn't going to give him up. He was one of her possessions. Melissa and her father owned him, and she never gave away for free anything that belonged to her.

Through the grapevine, Kat had learned enough details to satisfy herself that Doug was justified in seeking love elsewhere. She just wished it hadn't been with her.

She had forgiven him for much of what happened that night. But the one thing she would not, could not, forgive was the humiliation she had suffered because of him. It was still her weak point—and her strong point. Her pride was everything. Her father often told her she had too much of it for her own good. It was the one thing she could not tolerate anyone tampering with. And that is exactly what Doug Hayden had done that night and had tried to do this afternoon in front of the other reporters. He had tried to humiliate her again, and she was not going to stand for it. She would forgive him all else but that.

"Grown up?" She repeated his hope of her having done so. It was a rhetorical question, not meant to be answered. "Yes, I have grown up." She shifted uncomfortably on the bed, not wanting to discuss the burdensome weight that hung between them, making friendship an impossibility. "I suppose I have you to thank for that."

"I tried to call you after my divorce, Katherine." He leaned toward her, almost reaching out to touch her arm, but his hand stopped in midair when he saw her jerk away. "I wanted to tell you that I really did—"

"There's not much point in discussing the matter now, Doug." Kat couldn't stand thinking about the event, much less talking about it. Why was he here, bringing it all back again? Did he have a guilty conscience? She certainly hoped so. But still, she knew that it was more than guilt; he wanted her to go easy on him in her articles. She could tell now that what she wrote really did affect him. The realization gave her a feeling of power over him, and that made her feel good. "It happened, and that's all there is to it. Now, we both really do need to get some sleep, however little. So why don't we just say good night."

She climbed off the bed, ready to battle any attempts he might have of making her stay there. For a split second she felt a sharp sense of disappointment when he offered no argument. He raised himself slowly from the bed, donned his golf hat, and set the two champagne glasses on her counter.

She didn't, couldn't, look at him, but she knew he was watching her, waiting for a reaction or hoping for some sign that they could once again be something more than enemies. She stared at the carpeting and watched his feet move across its gray pile toward the door. She followed behind him, so that she could close and lock the door after him.

He turned around abruptly, and she glanced up, startled by the intense gleam in his eyes. When he grasped the back of her head with his large hand, she stiffened, but he pulled her easily to him and, lowering his head, branded her lips with his own. His tongue found the center of her mouth, and, though there was reluctancy in her movement, Kat's own tongue reached out to stroke the tip of his. There was fire in his kiss, and it burned a searing path through her bloodstream.

When he pulled away he smiled crookedly, saying, "Good night . . . friend."

She watched him walk away into the darkness, and only

after he was long beyond her sight did she regain enough composure to close and lock the door.

Friend! That was no friendly kiss. Her own rapid heartbeat and aching loins said that it was much, much more.

She glanced over at her typewriter on the floor by the bed, in hopes that through it she might find some way to drive his demon from her. She had to get her mind back on the right track, back to the task of deflating Doug's self-importance, of making him pay for her humiliation. But even the thought of lambasting him with some cruel "scoop" brought no ease to her mind this night.

In a daze, she walked back to the bed and curled her tired body onto the warm spot where, only a moment earlier, Doug had lain. Falling immediately to sleep, Kat absorbed the substance of his strong, hard body into her dreams.

CHAPTER FOUR

The sun was at a thirty-degree angle before Kat awakened. She had intended to rise early and maybe catch some of the golfers as they were starting out on their rounds. But since the night had brought an unexpected abridgment of sleep, it was all Kat could do to drag herself out of bed.

As quickly as her still-tired body would allow, she donned her jeans, Pierre Cardin T-shirt, and canvas-soled sandals. She was in the habit of wearing very little makeup in the daytime, so after brushing on a little mascara and applying some lip gloss, then fastening her hair back at the sides with blue barettes, she was ready to go. The thought of eating breakfast after drinking champagne in the middle of the night threw her stomach into a sea of nausea.

Had she dreamed what took place last night? Had it been the dragon of her conscience coming to haunt her? It was the first time she had had any close, personal contact with Doug since that night in Kansas City so long ago. She had avoided him at all costs during the two years she had followed the Tour. In fact, her only interaction with him at all had been on the typewritten page. There, she had said the things she would have liked to say to his face if she had had the nerve.

Last night changed nothing! Why did she feel that she

had to emphasize that to her own mind? So he kissed her. Big deal! But, damn it, why did she have to kiss him back? How could he still make her respond to him after so much time had elapsed? It was disgusting! He wasn't the only fish in the sea. Last night was a mistake, but it was one that would not be repeated again. She would make sure of that.

As she stepped outside the van she was assaulted by a rolling wave of heat. It was only nine thirty in the morning, and already the air was stifling. Stepping back into the van, she grabbed a golf hat, figuring she would need it that afternoon to shield her face from the blazing sun.

After saying good-bye to Bogie and locking the van, Kat headed for the press tent. There was a reluctancy in her step that hadn't been there yesterday, and she couldn't help but wonder at her slight hesitation.

The press tent was only about half full of journalists, the others already out on the course with those golfers who had early tee-off times.

Kat looked around the tent for Tim but couldn't find him anywhere. He must have had a late night with his blond friend, she surmised with pursed lips. Spotting Paul in the corner, she walked over to where he was typing frantically away.

"Have you got a big story already?" Kat's voice sounded somewhat incredulous.

"Are you kidding! I'm just working on one that was supposed to be finished last week." Paul cursed as he hit the wrong key. Erasing his error, he continued typing as if Kat weren't there. "If you're looking for Tim, he's following Cramer and Bradshaw. They teed off at . . . let's see . . . eight thirty, I think."

"Okay, thanks. Maybe I'll catch up with him later."

Kat walked over to the ice box and pulled out a Coke. Popping the top, she drank deeply, hoping the carbonation would settle her queasy stomach somewhat. Walking back to Paul, she asked, "Who are you going to follow?"

"Hayden," he answered, without looking up from his typewriter. "He tees off in about fifteen minutes."

Kat sighed without comment, looking around the tent for an escape from this pit she felt she was about to fall into. "Maybe I'll tag along, too." What made her say that! Why on earth would she want to follow Doug Hayden around the course! She had planned to follow Watson and Trevino. Well, she could still follow them. She didn't have to follow Doug.

But, fifteen minutes later, when Paul clicked off his typewriter and headed for the number one tee to watch Doug Hayden begin his round, Kat was right behind.

A large gallery had already gathered at the tee mound to watch their hero with the magic swing hit his first drive of the day. As soon as he walked onto the tee box, excitement rippled through the crowd. Golf was essentially a quiet sport, requiring great concentration and an ebullience that always retained an undercurrent of civilized control. But Kat could still detect the electricity in the air and the flurry of anticipation running beneath the composed exteriors of the spectators as they observed Doug.

Watching Doug walk across the mound, bending to plant his tee in the grass, Kat felt a rushing current of excitement churn through her own body. It was a flutter of agitation that had nothing at all to do with the game, but everything to do with the sexual magnetism of the man on the tee box.

Doug was dressed in khaki-colored pants and a navy-

and-rust knit shirt, and Kat's eyes were drawn once again to the lines of his body, where the clothes hugged the muscles beneath.

Lifting his head to crack a joke with his caddie, Kat saw the flash of white teeth against Doug's tan face and felt a warm glow that radiated from her toes, spreading up through her legs and curling in the pit of her stomach.

Shaking her head to dispel the hypnotic state she had entered at the sight of him, Kat tried to concentrate on the day's game.

Two of the three other players in the foursome had been playing well this year and would probably make the cut the following night. She had overheard several of the men in the press tent making bets over Tom Billings and Will Granshaw, so both of those men would be worth watching very closely this day and the next. Kat could at least rationalize that she was not following Doug, but was following the other two instead. Though it helped to ease her own self-disgust a bit, she knew she was lying to herself. This was Doug's kind of golf course—lots of rolls, several doglegs to the right, which he had perfected over the years—and some uncontrollable emotion deep inside of Kat was rooting for him to win.

The noise in the crowd had died to a soft whisper. Holding his club behind the ball, Doug leaned over slightly, every muscle of his body braced in concentration. Slowly pulling the club back high over his shoulder, he paused only for a second, then swung through the ball with a force that left Kat breathless. When the club struck the ball a sharp crack registered in the air, followed by a rising hum of awe from the crowd behind. The ball sailed straight through the air, flying parallel to the ground down the center of the fairway, then dropped heavily to the soft grass of the fairway almost two hundred and twenty-five yards away.

Doug watched with narrowed eyes until his ball landed safely where he had intended for it to land, then turned his head to wink at Kat. Not realizing he had even noticed her in the crowd, she was stunned by his gesture of familiarity. Stiffening her spine, she stared back at him with what she hoped was a look of complete lack of interest.

Chuckling to himself over some private joke, Doug handed his caddie his club and turned to watch the other three players tee off.

Maybe she should just stay here and wait for the next foursome. She didn't have to follow this one, she reminded herself. But, as soon as the last player drove his ball down the center of the fairway and the crowd began to move, Kat was carried along with them, her eyes never leaving Doug's back as he walked down the fairway, chatting with some reporters and spectators to his left.

The day had started off well for Doug Hayden. By the third hole he was two under par and his crowd of followers had doubled. It was only the first day of the tournament, but because of the star-studded quality of this golf classic, network television cameras were already following Doug's every move, and soft-spoken announcers verbalized the action for home viewers.

On the fourth hole, Doug's ball was lying thirty-five feet from the flag, a sand bunker between his ball and the green. With a chip and one putt he would par the hole, thus retaining a two-under score. If it took three shots, he would bogey the hole and drop a point in his overall score. Though it was still early in the match, the pressure was on to grab an early lead and retain it throughout the day.

Looking as relaxed as if he were out for a leisurely practice round, Doug stepped up to the ball. The only outward sign that he was feeling the pressure was in the involuntary flexing of his strong jaw muscles.

Kat didn't realize that her palms were sweating and that she was clenching and unclenching her hands repeatedly at her sides.

Pulling his nine iron back at a forty-five-degree angle, Doug swung through, lofting the ball gracefully up and over the bunker and the slight rise of the green, setting it down five feet from the flag, where it rolled as if drawn by a magnet to the edge of the hole and dropped inside.

Surprised and elated, Doug turned his smiling face to the now ecstatic gallery. Shrugging his shoulders, he commented, "What can I say?" and laughed.

"Did you see that!" Paul was wide-eyed with amazement over the shot.

"I saw it," Kat exclaimed. "But I don't believe it." An unexplainable surge of pride shot through her at the success of Doug's shot, and she smiled in bemusement at her reaction.

The mobile scorekeeper scratched out the minus two on the board, replacing it with a minus three. It looked as if it were going to be a good day for Doug Hayden.

Kat felt as though it were going to be a good day for her, too. But suddenly, on the fifth hole, her sense of euphoria came to a dramatic halt.

While Doug was feeling obviously ebullient over his game so far and cracking jokes right and left to the gallery, Kat had been swept along with the tide of adulation that lapped around his ankles.

On hole number five Doug had to contend with a sharp dogleg to the right, which he managed perfectly with his natural fade, the ball slicing gracefully around the edge of the trees. His second shot landed the ball in the sand trap to the left of the green. But with an easy chip shot he was on the green in three. Then all he had to do was nip the ball and drop it into the hole for a par.

A man, whom Kat thought she recognized but at this distance couldn't quite place, walked into Doug's line of vision. The eyes of the two men locked for only an instant. But it seemed to Kat that in that instant, a volume of words were spoken. As quickly as he had appeared, the man donned a bright-yellow cap and walked back into the gallery, fading from view.

Doug scowled briefly as he watched the man walk away. Then, with a new look of determination, he smiled to himself as he walked over to putt his ball into the hole. Before he hit the ball he glanced up at Kat, feigning a look of complete surprise, as though he were seeing her for the first time that day.

Smiling wickedly, he purred, "Did you sleep well after —after I left this morning, love?" Knowing full well that every camera and microphone was directed on him, Doug grinned like a cat with canary feathers still hanging out of his mouth, and walked over to his ball. With an effortless putt he dropped it into the hole.

Kat did not budge. Every muscle, every nerve in her body, was shocked into immovability. For that brief moment every camera and every face in the crowd around them had been focused on her reddened face, wondering, speculating, drawing their own conclusions to Doug's remark. Holding back the shudder of indignation that threatened to ripple through her, Kat felt the heat of intense curiosity from Paul's eyes as he stared at her.

God! Doug had done it again! He had humiliated her in

front of hundreds of people, national television cameras, and her fellow journalists!

Trying to regain her composure even though she knew there were those around her staring and smiling to themselves, Kat forced her eyes up and, from across the green, glared at Doug with a scowl so intense, a rage so fomenting and explosive, it could have turned granite into molten lava.

As the crowd moved over to the sixth tee, Kat stayed behind, her eyes boring into Doug's back with the penetrating thrust of a dozen well-honed daggers.

Standing alone beside the green, she inwardly cursed the name of Doug Hayden with enough coarse imprecations to make a sailor cringe like a schoolboy. Then she said aloud, "You'll be sorry for this, Doug. If I have to follow you to my dying day, I'll make you pay for your warped sense of humor." Already she was formulating the words that would eventually bring him to his knees.

The heat had not abated in the slightest. Even though it was six o'clock, and the sun had dipped low in the western sky, there was a thick stillness in the air that was suffocating. Several hours before, Kat had pulled her hair high atop her head, securing it as best she could with the two barettes she had with her. A few wavy tendrils defied control and were stuck to her neck and temples from the dampness. Her T-shirt clung to her skin like flypaper, and she vowed she would never wear another pair of blue jeans again.

Those were the exterior signs of discomfort. Inside, she was still seething with a heat that made the outside temperature of her body seem like an arctic cold mass in comparison.

After her debilitating humiliation on the number five green, she lagged behind to follow another foursome. She knew that by all appearances she was letting Doug win, but she couldn't bear the thought of having people stare at her anymore. It was so embarrassing!

The euphoric glow of this tournament had suddenly grown cold, and it was going to be all she could do to make it through the next few days.

As she dragged her way to the press tent, Kat passed the scoreboard to her left. The results of the day's round screamed at her tauntingly. Doug was three strokes ahead of all the other players, and he now sat at eight under par for the first eighteen holes. It seemed like the final blow to her already rotten day.

Making her way through the throng of people, she was oblivious to the stares of curiosity she was receiving. It was only when a sports reporter for one of the major television networks stepped up with his microphone and asked her to clarify the relationship between herself and Doug Hayden that she almost lost control.

She smiled sweetly. "For the record, sir, there is no—I repeat, no—relationship between Doug Hayden and myself. There never has been. There never will be. This is obviously his idea of a cute joke. But as it comes from a warped mind, it can only be taken in that context." Then, clamping her hand tightly over his microphone, she barked, "And, if I hear one more word about Doug Hayden or myself, I'm going to tell you, on live television, exactly what you can do with that microphone of yours. Now, if you'll excuse me . . ."

Angrily Kat shoved her way through the milling crowd and onward to the insulating safety of the press tent. However, once she reached the interior, she was bombarded with questions from all sides about Doug's innuendo. Had they indeed had a rendezvous last night? How long had their relationship been going on? Were they planning marriage? Would this affect his career? Her career?

Out of the field of faces one friendly pillar of strength and security emerged. Reaching through the reporters, Tim clasped Kat's hand, pulling her toward him. Rescuing her from the barrage of questions, he led her out into the evening heat, past spectators who continued to linger on the course, and on out across the empty fairways.

Shaking from the physical and psychological torment of the confrontation with the mob of reporters, it was several minutes before Kat could calm her breathing enough to speak.

"Tim—I—thank you—God, thank you." She was gasping for air, but the stifling tropical heat that filled her lungs was enough to suffocate her.

"Slow down, Kat. Calm yourself, okay?" Tim's steady voice soothed the tumultuous thoughts in her mind, and soon her pulse was beating at a slower, more even rate.

Stopping under a large oak tree, Kat plopped to the ground, fatigue defying any attempts to move. She lay back against the soft grass and gazed up through the branches draped with Spanish moss.

Tim leaned back against the trunk and watched her, waiting for her to collect herself enough to talk.

Sighing, she glanced over at him and groaned. "Do you believe this?"

"I'm not sure. Do you want to talk about it?"

"There really isn't anything to talk about!" she almost shouted. "Oh, damn, he's even got me yelling at you." She sniffed in disgust at the situation. "Last night, or rather this morning, about two, Doug came to my van. He had

had more than enough to drink, and he had this crazy idea that we should be friends. You see"—Kat sat up and turned to face Tim—"three years ago, we—we almost had a relationship. It was when I was playing the amateur circuit, and I was teamed with him for a pro-am match. I guess I kind of . . . fell for him. But that was before I found out he was married. Found out the hard way, you might say. Anyway, it was really . . . no big thing."

She sensed a flicker of disbelief in Tim's eyes, but it was quickly masked over with his concern for her.

"I was shocked totally when he came to the van last night. The only reason I can think of is that he wants to get me off his back. He's very hot on himself right now and likes reading all the garbage that's printed about him. The touch of reality I throw in is obviously something he doesn't want to face." The muscles in Kat's face were tightening involuntarily as she thought of what Doug was doing to her. "He's trying to ruin me, Tim!"

There was a long moment's pause before Tim commented, "Isn't that what you're trying to do to him, Kat?"

With a look of stunned disbelief Kat stared at Tim. "No—I—I'm just trying to be a writer. I can't help it if I see Doug as something less than everyone else sees him." Kat didn't notice the tensely guarded expression that suddenly covered Tim's face. "He's just a man, Tim. He's not—"

"I guess I should be grateful that you realize that." Kat looked sharply at Tim, but his mouth had not moved. Spinning around, she was met by Doug's towering frame above her. He was standing with one foot crossed over the other, his weight leaning against a putter in his right hand. With his left hand he tossed a golf ball repeatedly into the air, never failing to catch it even though his eyes were trained on Kat's face. There was fatigue written into the planes of his face, but Kat was too startled and angry to notice.

"Is there no place I can go where I'm safe from you?" she sneered.

"We have to talk, Katherine." His eyes never left her face, but Tim took the cue, standing, with an apologetic glance at Kat, then strolled back across the fairway toward the parking lot.

Standing and brushing off any grass from the back of her jeans, Kat glared at Doug. "There is absolutely nothing that we have to say to each other." She pivoted away from him and started to walk in the direction Tim had gone.

Doug's hand, like a steel vise, clamped around her arm. There was no pain in the grip, but she felt a strength that she knew she could not fight. Turning her around to face him, Doug repeated, "We have to talk."

Slowly exhaling her breath, she lowered her eyes to glare at the arm he held. When he loosened his hold she shrugged her arm away and begrudgingly began walking beside him farther out onto the course.

"About today, Katherine." He glanced over at her grim profile and sighed. "I didn't mean to cause any trouble for you. I really didn't."

"I'll bet," she snarled.

"Hey!" He grabbed both of her upper arms with his hands, the putter and ball poking into her muscles. "I have never in my life lied to a friend."

"Oh, excuse me." She began walking again, a restlessness to her stride. "I should have realized that the Tour's favorite son was also a boy scout."

"You just don't quit, do you, Katherine?" Doug's voice had a harsh edge to it now.

"Me!" She had to fight to keep from screaming at him at the top of her lungs. She stopped walking and turned to glare at him. "Don't you know what you've done to my career? Don't you realize that if everyone thinks you and I are . . . an item, I will have no credibility left as an objective journalist?"

"Nobody in their right mind is going to think that." His mouth quirked in disbelief.

"They will, Doug. You don't know how difficult it is for a woman in this field. Everyone is just waiting for me to screw up, and it looks like you've done that for me." Her eyes filmed over with defeat, and she swallowed hard to keep a lump from forming in her throat.

"I can't believe that just because of one little remark—Katherine, I had no idea you would be affected this way." He dropped the putter and ball to the ground and grasped her arms again, but this time with an intensity that left her breathless. "You've got to believe me. I never meant this to happen."

She stared at his unflinching gaze. The intensity of his feelings and the gathering darkness of approaching night had turned his eyes to a dark, smoky blue, and the look in them was one of honesty. She really did believe him.

"All I was doing was making a joke," he continued to explain. "I thought it would lighten up the situation a bit. You know me"—he shook his head as if disgusted with himself—"always the joker. Damn!" He thought for a minute. "Listen. Tomorrow I'll do whatever I can to set the record straight, okay?"

Without answering, Kat continued to watch his face with fascination. She had never seen him this way. When he said he was sorry there was a stark frankness etched into his features. His eyes never left her face, and she watched as they grew soft and warm in the waning summer light.

She was drawn to something in the depths of those eyes, pulled deep into the hidden pools beneath the surface. Her vision was filled by the light in them, leaving room for nothing else. It was the same reaction she had had toward him three years ago. It was the same and it was different. Then, she had been blind to what was beneath the surface, dazzled only by the exterior attraction. Now she sensed something more, something stronger and more compelling in Doug Hayden than she ever had dreamed of.

"I had a good day today, Katherine, and I want to share it with you. Please don't leave yet."

As if right on cue in a scenario, they both moved toward each other, their arms reaching out to enclose one another. As Doug's arms pulled her against his hard frame, she felt a shudder of longing so intense, her knees almost collapsed. Desire flooded her mind and body, and she sensed, rather than saw, his mouth descending unerringly onto hers. As he gently moved his mouth over her lips, exploring their outline, she felt a hot glow spreading through her veins.

She welcomed the growing intensity of his mouth, parting her lips to take his tongue into her mouth and taste its sweetness. The roughness of it against her own tongue sent a raging fire through her stomach and legs. She couldn't get enough. She grasped the back of his hair and pulled him harder against her. He reacted by pressing her hips with his hand, pulling her against his hard thighs.

Their hands were set loose in a torrent of caresses. Her hands moved down from his hair, one massaging his neck while the other pressed at the base of his spine and then climbed slowly upward, her fingers curling into the knit cloth on his back.

His large hands moved boldly across her jean-clad hips, pulling her ever tighter against the growing urgency of his desire. His right hand dipped under her shirt and spread across the warm skin of her back. Unclasping her bra, he gently wedged his hand beneath it, grasping her breast and stroking the tip with his thumb.

"God!" he breathed against her mouth. Trailing kisses across her face, he buried his mouth in her hair, his breath warm and tantalizing against her scalp.

With a fluidity that felt no physical restraints, they were pulled to the ground by the gravitation of their desire. Lost in a world of sensations beyond reason, they lay in the soft grass at the edge of a green, protected against all eyes by the mossy elevated slope above them.

The red-hued sky had melted into darkness without either of them being aware of the sun's passage beyond the horizon. Night gathered around and clothed them in its protective custody.

They were in a bed of moss, a sea of green, rolling and rising, lofting to heights beyond imagination. Without regard for finesse, Kat helped Doug remove his shirt, and he then lifted her shirt over her shoulders and, with what seemed almost like impatience, tore the loosened bra from her arms.

Before he could remove her jeans, she pulled him down on top of her, and between the bare skin of her breasts against his hair-covered chest was an electrical storm of current so full of fire that they were wrapped in the bliss of it alone for several minutes. His mouth trailed kisses down the hollow of her throat, his tongue blazing a path across her skin to her breasts. His tongue circled each nipple in turn again and again, and she felt herself rising to take more of whatever he would give her.

His left hand grasped a handful of her hair, and his mouth opened wider over her breasts, sending shock waves coursing through her body.

Lying to the side of her, with one leg draped across her thighs, he began slowly to unfasten the zipper and snap of her jeans. His hand played across the silken front of her panties and dipped under one leg band, where it hugged her thigh. Her mind reeled with the intoxicating scents of the night and the man, and with the overwhelming need she had for him.

"What the hell . . . !"

As if being thrown suddenly into a frigid shower, the stinging shock of rain began to pelt their half-clothed bodies. Stunned and dazed over what was happening, they both sat up quickly, Doug wrapping her in the fold of his arms for protection.

Looking around, he uttered a harsh expletive that spoke the sentiments of both of them. They were lying on the side of the tenth green, and all around were spewing showers of water, sprayed into the air from the underground sprinkler system.

In a less intense situation, it might have been funny. But neither of them was laughing. Burying her head against Doug's chest, Kat tried to calm her ragged breathing. His fingers combed through her hair and seemed reluctant to stop.

Finally finding the strength to stand, they donned their shirts, and Kat fastened her jeans. At a brisk walk, they moved from the water's direct line of fire. However, they saw before them the fountains springing up across the entire course, so they began to run, Doug's free hand pulling Kat along at his speed. His other hand held the putter, but the ball was left to lie on the green, a gift to whoever might find it.

With only one thought in both of their minds, they ran in the direction of Kat's van. At least there they would not have to contend with untimely sprinklers.

Just as they were reaching the parking lot, they were halted by a group of players, all under the influence of postgame libations. Grabbing Doug away from Kat, they all began shouting and talking at once, wondering where he had been and why he was wet. They had been waiting for him to join the party that was planned at someone's hotel room and, grasping Kat's arm, insisted that she too join the celebration.

With all the commotion it was hard to make sense of any of it. But, slowly, the taunts and jibes of several in the group penetrated the numb sectors of her brain.

"So this is the little fireball reporter you've been talking about."

"This is Kath—" Doug tried to introduce her, but he was tossed about roughly in congratulations over his victory that day.

A voice from somewhere inside Kat began to scream: No! I can't ruin my career over one incident! Tell them, Doug! You promised you would set the record straight. Tell them!

Someone in the crowd jeered, "Do you always soften him up this way before shooting him down with your cynical reviews, honey?"

Kat stared at Doug, her eyes filled with the painful need for them all to know the truth about her relationship with him. But what was her relationship really? And what did she want him to say? She didn't want to become involved with him. It would be the end of her career. And she wanted that too badly to give it up. But she also wanted . . .

Doug watched Kat's eyes, and though he couldn't fathom the meaning behind them, he was struck by the almost desperate appeal in them, and he remembered what he had told her. He promised that he would set the record straight. He would.

"Listen, you guys, please! Hey!" It took several long minutes before he could get their attention. "What I implied today on number five . . . about Miss Ingles and myself. That . . . that was a joke. There is nothing . . ." His eyes bore into Kat's face, searching for the truth of what she felt, what she wanted. Seeing only the determined jaw and darkened irises of her green eyes, he continued. ". . . absolutely nothing between Miss Ingles and me."

Staring vacantly into the circle of people, she vaguely heard attempts to get her to join them at the party. She watched as Doug was being dragged away, the hero of the day, his head turning only once to look at her. She was remotely aware of it all, and yet the only thing that was clear in her mind were the words ". . . absolutely nothing between Miss Ingles and me."

There was no vagueness there, no lack of clarity, no misinterpretation. And the sound of the pronouncement played over and over and over again in her head.

CHAPTER FIVE

It was funny how life moved forward, how nothing in nature paused to reflect on the pain of one of its creatures.

On Friday morning a light rain brought refreshing relief from the heat, the sky then clearing and remaining cloudless and blue for the remainder of the tournament.

There could have been a blizzard for all Kat noticed. The storm of feelings inside her own mind and body could be relieved by no amount of fair weather.

The unthinkable had happened again. How many times was she to come within a touch away of knowing Doug Hayden? She had never wanted anything so badly in her life. It wasn't just the need to experience the possession of a man, any man—it was to have Doug. No others had ever tempted her enough for her to want to share that experience with them.

Maybe it was because Doug was the first to have ever come so close. Or maybe it was because he represented "the unattainable." No, she knew it was neither. It was true, he had been the first to fill Kat with the overwhelming desire to make love. Others had tried before, but she was too much the perfectionist, finding flaws in all of them, too full of pride and ambition to let simple physical urges carry her away. Only Doug had been able to do that.

Only he had taken her down from her chaste white horse and shown her that there was more, much more, to life than external goals. Through him, she had been given a taste of the physical side of her being, made aware of her own sexuality, a side she never realized was so important to her overall character.

Oh, she had urges like any other normal young woman, but she had always been able to keep them in check. It was only after meeting Doug and being with him that night, which seemed so long ago, that she realized her life would never have a completeness without him.

The most bitter pill to swallow had been that making love to Doug was an impossibility. She had convinced herself that she would never do so. After all, he was a married man. Even after she learned of his divorce, she knew it would never happen. She had been too humiliated that night ever to forgive him to the point where she would sleep with him. It was inconceivable! She hated him!

Only after seeing him again at this tournament, after being so close to him, did the physical desires of her body claim authority over her rational emotional and mental states.

They had come so close. If only she could, just once, satisfy her physical craving for him, maybe she could drive his magical spell away. Maybe then she would no longer need to limit herself to him. She could then choose the man she wanted to live with forever, to have children with, to share her goals with. Not this sandy-haired, all-American golf bum. Her dream man would probably be the dark-haired, mysterious type, not one who had the open, honest look of a boy scout. And the man she chose in the end would never, ever, remember a single joke! That would be requirement number one! No more comedians.

For the next two days Kat avoided Doug at all costs, concentrating on the two interviews she had been promised at the dinner the first night of the tournament, and on the development of the tournament in general.

By Saturday night Doug's lead had slipped to only two strokes. Three players were at six under par, and four others were between three and five under. The pressure was on.

"What in the hell has happened to Hayden?" Kat was sitting at McDonald's, having dinner with Tim, Paul, and John. The three men were discussing the day's events, and their disappointment in Doug was clearly evident.

"I don't know," Paul said. "But I can't figure out which was worse today, his golf game or his attitude. Did you notice the change in him?"

Both Tim and Kat remained silent during this interchange, each with their own ideas as to what was the matter with Doug.

"Yes, I've noticed," John agreed. "He won't even talk to reporters. He seems to have forgotten how to smile, and the gallery just about gave up waiting for one of his jokes."

It was true. Doug had become less and less at ease with the crowds, more serious and thoughtful, no longer cracking one-liners between putts. His mood had grown from sour to grim, and by the end of the day he was talking to no one.

"You've talked to him quite a bit, Kat. What do you think is wrong?" Paul was watching her carefully, waiting to hear what she would say. After hearing Doug's remark Thursday on the number five green and seeing the effect it had had on Kat, Paul couldn't help but be suspicious of the relationship. It was true that, to anyone who approached him about it, Doug had made it very clear that his remark had been strictly a joke. There was no relationship between them. However, Paul still had his doubts. And he couldn't help but feel that whatever was wrong with Doug was somehow Kat's fault.

"I really haven't the faintest idea, Paul," Kat answered snidely, perturbed with him for believing other than what she had been denying. "Maybe it's an old war injury acting up," she added petulantly.

"I heard he's having some financial difficulties," John said.

"Oh, bull," Tim argued. "Hayden's got more money than he knows what to do with."

"Anyone who makes more money on one tournament than we make in a full year is hardly having financial difficulties," Kat remarked before biting hard into her hamburger, chewing automatically, without tasting the flavor of it at all.

"And he has all those endorsements and commercials and magazine ads," Paul added. "No, I bet it's some personal problems at home or something. But then, who can tell." He peered knowingly at Kat.

"I wish I could tell," John admitted. "I could sure use an exclusive story right now."

None of the comments about Doug's problems were allowed a niche in which to root in Kat's mind. She didn't care what his problems were. She had enough of her own, not the least of which was reestablishing her credibility as an unbiased golf reporter.

Doug's denial of a relationship between them had squelched most of the rumors, but she still noticed the skeptical stares, raised eyebrows, and occasional under-the-breath remarks that were directed toward her from some of the other journalists, especially from Paul and John.

On Sunday morning Kat made a concentrated effort to watch the scoreboard with a blank mind. She refused to let Doug's score affect her in the least. So what if he won or lost. She couldn't care less who came out on top. Had she been a woodcarver's son, her nose might have stretched from Florida to New York from all the lies she told herself.

By Sunday afternoon Doug had regained his momentum, ending up the final round of the tournament with a one stroke lead and a score of eight under par.

All Kat wanted now that the tournament was over was to get away from here. As soon as the press conference with the top five players was over, Kat stowed her typewriter and gear under her bed and started the van's engine.

As she pulled out of the parking lot she saw Doug leaning over the trunk of his car, angrily throwing his golf bag into it. When Kat's van passed he looked up, and their eyes locked for what seemed an eternal, time-stopping moment. To see her, he had to face the sun, and his eyes and nose and mouth were pinched into tight lines that revealed nothing of what he was thinking.

Pressing her foot to the accelerator, Kat drove out onto the main road and did not look back. She had read nothing in his expression that would make her turn back. Ever.

Kat stood up from the couch, pulling the sheet of paper out of the typewriter, wadding it into a tight ball, and pitching it onto the pile of crumpled-up paper balls that overflowed the trash basket.

Stretching her arms high over her head, then lowering them and kneading the small of her back with her fingers, she walked to the open door of the van. Stepping down onto the beach, she let her mind rest, ceasing all stressful thoughts, relishing instead the pure sensation of her toes digging into the cool, moist sand.

Night stretched across the beach, lending a sense of quiet, of peace, that was almost out of place here. During the day Daytona Beach roared with souped-up hot rods, exhaled the combined odors of saltwater fish, steaming coney dogs, and acrid marijuana, and clamored with the boisterous din of the youthful crowds.

But with the sunbathers and swimmers all gone, and the smells of the day with them, Kat could breathe in the fragrance of the ocean. The waves at night seemed much larger and louder than in the daytime, their crashing dance upon the sand reverberating long after the tide had pulled the breakers back into its folds.

Kat had been here for three days. It was her fourth night to sleep on the beach. Leaving the moment the tournament was over, she had made it to Daytona just as the sun was cresting over the horizon. She needed a rest. She needed to think. Maybe she had been traveling too much lately. Maybe she had seen too many golf matches.

She needed to sit back and reevaluate what she was doing with her life. If nothing else, the days on the beach were to give her the time to work on a couple of articles.

The tournament had been a disaster, saved only by the two interviews she had been promised. She got some great quotes and some new insight into the controversy over handicaps for the Tour pros. So why, in heaven's name, couldn't she get it down on paper correctly? She had been typing for three solid days, and still she had nothing to show for it. What was the matter with her?

It was that demon, Doug Hayden. Every time she stared

at the paper in the typewriter, a vision of that sandy-haired, suntanned man with the boyish grin winked back at her. Why couldn't she exorcise him once and for all from her mind? Was it always to be this way? Was she to be forever tormented by an image of his strong, tan body leaning over her, his mouth and tongue touching every sensitive nerve in her body? Surely all she needed was a man, any man. But the thought of lying next to anyone else but Doug left her body feeling numb, a trackless void of sensation. Her pulse did not accelerate at the thought, her skin did not tingle. She felt no quivering tremors in her stomach. It was no good. Nothing she did or thought about would erase Doug's searing brand from her mind.

She had her pick of images of him to choose from. There was the disciplined, commanding Doug on the tee mound, swinging his club effortlessly through the ball, his eyes squinting into the sun as he calmly surveyed his impressive shot. There was the laughing Doug, passing off a witty one-liner to a fan in the crowd or bantering back and forth good-naturedly with his caddie. And there was the sexual Doug and the memory of his hard body pressing her into the grass, his mouth bringing her to heights of pleasure beyond even those found in her dreams.

Though all of the images stood before her in painful, crystal clarity, it was the sexual image that haunted Kat the most: the quietly seductive man who displayed no need to flaunt his masculine magnetism; the selfless giver of pleasure, whose own needs and wants were blatantly evident in his response to her enjoyment. This was the Doug who tormented her dreams, stole her sleep and her appetite. This was the Doug she knew she must stay away from.

Pulling in a tortured breath of frustration, she flung

each of the images of him into the night, out over the water, where they would drop into the ocean forever and drown.

Turning around to reenter the lighted van, she sighed in dismay. There they were. All three images were before her, the most haunting one, the sexual man, in front of all the others, with eyes that impaled her with their direct invitation, with their crystal-blue persuasion.

She sighed, closing the door on the beach, seeing nothing ahead but another night of sleepless torment.

She was aware that Doug would be playing in a tournament the following week in North Carolina. He was a man driven to play continuously, completing thirty-six events last year and never complaining about the demanding grind of the Tour. Yes, he would be there next week, there was no doubt about that. But Kat would not.

By Thursday noon she had finished one article, and, though she wasn't totally satisfied with it, she stuffed it with a cover letter into an envelope and addressed it to the editor of one of the golf magazines.

Kat knew she should try to work on another one, but she couldn't seem to concentrate. She had this restless feeling, this need to move on, to— No! She wasn't going to North Carolina. She began taking the sheets and cover from her bed and stuffing them into the storage area beneath. She wasn't going to put herself through that torture again. She folded the bed back into the couch position. She had just about had it with golf. She walked the length of the van, checking to make sure that each cabinet was latched. There was certainly no way she was going to go to the tournament with Doug there.

Bogie lay in a captain's chair, licking his front paws, unmindful of whether they stayed or went. She would only be setting herself up for more heartache if she went. She sat in the driver's seat, clicking the ignition over. The engine began to hum, and the sudden turning over of the motor startled some sunbathers a few feet away. Doug had humiliated her enough, and she couldn't take any more. The van, as if under a will of its own, threw sand from under its turning wheels and turned onto the highway, heading north.

If she was going to North Carolina, it would probably take her about twelve hours to get there. But then, it didn't matter, because she wasn't going there anyway.

As she eased the van into an empty parking space, her gaze scanned the country-club setting. The golf course curved and undulated under a heavy canopy of pine trees. The course in Florida had been wide and open, bathed in a yellow glow. But here in North Carolina, Kat drank in the cool peacefulness of the shady fairways and greens. It would be a pleasant change of environment, a change she needed desperately, she told herself.

Stepping out of the van, she paused, letting the cool breeze brush against the exposed skin of her face, neck, and arms. Slinging her tote bag over her shoulder, she headed for the press tent, praying that she would be able to talk her way into a pass.

At the entrance gate, she was stopped by the guard.

"My credentials, parking sticker, and badge are in the press tent," she said, smiling sweetly.

Whether it was her smile or his own gullibility, the guard believed her and let her enter. Now all she had to do was convince the tournament director to give her a badge.

Stepping up to the table where the officials sat, Kat

breathed deeply and began, "I forgot to send away for my credentials, and I was hoping that I could have a badge made up here."

The director stared at her for a long moment, trying to judge what this girl was trying to pull. Was she a golf groupie? They had certainly had their share of those. No. She looked a little too sure of herself for that. Maybe a wife or ex-wife checking up on late alimony payments.

"Well, if it isn't our roving redheaded reporter." Frank Willis stepped up and draped his arm across Kat's shoulder.

"You know this woman?" the director asked.

"Yeah, she's harmless enough. What'd ya do, Kat, forget your badge? Tsk, tsk."

As obnoxious as Frank was, she had to admit she was grateful for his interference at that moment. His fat arm and big mouth had just saved the day.

"How do you spell your name?" the director asked in a monotone voice.

"Kat, K-a-t. Ingles, I-n-g-l-e-s."

He typed her name on a badge and handed it to her grudgingly, thinking how strange it was that he had misread her. He was usually such a good judge of character.

Loosening herself from Frank's clutches, Kat tossed her tote bag onto an empty seat in the corner. She didn't want any questions, any conversation. She just wanted to get some interviews, watch a little golf, and then head out again. It was a simple enough goal. So why did it suddenly seem so unattainable?

An image rose in her mind. It was of a sandy-haired man swinging a golf club, then turning two crystal-blue eyes toward her, a half-smile playing around his lips.

Kat pivoted sharply in her chair, certain that she would

catch him standing behind her, a devilish grin on his face. But there was a vision full of emptiness, a sight filled with dark-green pine trees and sloping fairways, but lacking the one, essential ingredient that would bring the view to life.

Sighing, she shifted her attention to the pairing sheet in her hands, making note of Doug's tee-off time that afternoon.

CHAPTER SIX

A large crowd had begun to gather around the mound of the number one tee. The humming sounds of conversation, laughter, and excitement that scattered through the gallery all faded beneath the wild singing inside Kat's ears as Doug walked onto the tee mound. He was wearing navy slacks and a yellow knit shirt with navy and burgundy stripes. The yellow collar boldly highlighted the gold streaks in his hair. In the shade of the pine trees, his blue eyes were cool and direct. But the shadows of the trees also caused a different look in them that Kat did not remember having seen before, a hardness that she thought would surely dissipate when they were touched once again by the full glow of the sun.

He was taking some practice swings while the other players in the foursome took turns driving their balls down the fairway. As Doug swung, Kat watched the play of muscles in his shoulders and arms. When his fingers wrapped tightly around the shaft of his club, the backs of her knees weakened with the remembrance of that grip on her arms, and her pulse jumped fitfully.

Finishing his practice swings, he leaned his weight against the shaft and focused his eyes on the player now shooting.

From across the tee box he saw her. The breeze was throwing her red hair into wild disarray. He watched as she pulled some strands away from her face, and he was struck by the touch of vulnerability in her eyes. He wanted to reach out and brush the hair from her face, touching her skin with his fingers.

Kat saw him stiffen suddenly, then realized that it was she he had seen across the tee box.

Their eyes locked. His, like cool blue polestars, were drawing her sea-green ones into his magnetic field.

There was a moment of surprised stillness, when everything around them moved in a wake of silence.

He was startled to see her, she could tell. But what other thoughts were in his mind she could not read, except . . . she was sure . . . positive . . . she read desire in his eyes . . . hopefulness.

It was, for those few breath-quickening moments, as if time existed for them alone. But the moment was over as quickly as it had begun, and Kat was to wonder if it had existed in reality or only in her mind.

As Doug stepped to the center of the tee box and bent to place his tee in the ground, the tension in the crowd was tangible. Wrapping his fingers around the club with a tight grip, he pulled the driver back slowly, straightening his right knee as the club moved, then with swiftness and strength he pushed the club through the ball, hooking it around the angle of the dogleg and ending up with a perfect lie in the fairway. The crowd cheered enthusiastically, and Doug's mouth formed a happy grin.

Turning to face Kat, he smiled, a smile that spoke only to her and left her insides quaking with the eager tremors that pulsated through her. Inside, she fell apart. But she knew, in that moment, that whatever hook he had sunk into her flesh, whatever magic spell he had cast upon her body, she could not loosen his hold. As if her body and soul had no more substance than a hollow aluminum golf club, she was caught in his burning grip, the marrow of her bones liquefied by the heat of his strong hands.

By the end of Friday's eighteen holes, Doug had made the cut easily and was sharing the lead with one other player. Several others were one and two strokes behind, leaving the outcome of the next day's round a matter of guesswork.

The fans in North Carolina, oblivious to Doug Hayden's peculiar shift in mood at the Florida tournament, were content with the behavior of their easygoing hero. And the press seemed willing enough to forget his minor lapse, concentrating on the Doug with whom they were familiar.

While Kat stared at the electronic scoreboard, scribbling the scores on her notepad, she noticed Sam Calhoun, the player from Arkansas who had been a football hero in college and had only taken up the game of golf three years earlier.

Sam was what is known on the pro tour as a "rabbit," one of those rookies who had never won a tournament and who was required to play in a qualifying round the Monday before each tournament.

This was the first tournament this year in which he had made the cut, and Kat had once before mentioned to one of her editors that she would try and work up an article around him. Wanting to make sure she would get an interview, she pushed through the crowds, trying to reach him where he stood by the scoreboard.

A beer can in his hands and a satisfied beam on his face,

he smiled condescendingly at the pretty redhead who was trying to get his attention.

"Mr. Calhoun?" she inserted between comments of the fans who were gathered around him.

"Sam." He smiled a bit smugly as his insolent gaze traveled the length of her body.

"Sam," she began, trying to ignore the arrogance of his stare. "I'm Kat Ingles. I'm a free-lance writer, and—"

"Yes, I've heard of you." He folded his arms across his chest, his smile fading a little.

"I was wondering . . . if I might have a chance to talk to you about your shift from football to golf."

"Well, surely, honey," he drawled, draping his arm with familiarity around her shoulder, a gesture that Kat disliked almost as much as being called honey. "I'll tell you what," he whispered in her ear. "You come with me to a party we're having tonight, and I'll give you all the pretty little details you want."

"Mr. Calhoun—Sam." She was about to decline the invitation when she spotted Doug a few feet away. He was watching them curiously, taking note of every detail of the picture—Sam's arm around her shoulder, his mouth next to her ear—and an ice-cold look glazed over his eyes. Kat had a smile on her lips that faded at the sight of his expression. Had she misread his look on the tee this afternoon? Had she wanted him to want her and seen only what she wanted to see?

Without a word, Doug turned and disappeared into the crowd. She had misread him that afternoon. She had thought he cared. . . . God, what a fool she was! Well, to hell with him. She wasn't going to miss this chance at a story. She'd just go to the stupid party and get her damn story.

Turning to Sam, she smiled sweetly. "I'd love to go, Sam."

"Great, darlin'. It's at the hotel we're staying in, The Pines. Do you know where it is?"

"I'm sure I can find it." The arrogant bum wasn't even going to pick her up!

"Okay, eight o'clock. Room four-oh-nine."

What she had to go through to get a story. It wasn't fair! The other reporters didn't have to put up with this chauvinistic bull. Well, at least it would be a party, and she could perhaps talk to some other golfers and maybe, just maybe, forget about Doug Hayden for a few hours.

It was some party! A hundred people, it seemed, were packed into this large hotel suite. Drinks and noise were competing for center stage, and Kat wondered if she'd ever get an interview in this wild setting.

She had seen Sam only twice since she got there. He met her at the door, kissed her soundly on the mouth, and stuck a full beer can in her hands. A few minutes later he resurfaced with a "Sorry I can't spend more time with you, honey, but I gotta mingle. You don't mind, do you?"

"About that interview, Sam . . ."

"We'll get to it, darlin'. Don't you fret. We'll get to . . ." Once again she was alone, blessedly so, she had to admit.

Trying to move with the crowd, she became painfully aware of how this party was very much like the one she had been to so long ago in Kansas City. Golfers with their dates, their wives. They were all here, all but . . .

Before the name could form in her mind, he was standing before her. Raising her gaze above the shoulders of everyone else, she was met by two clear blue eyes that impaled her with a sharp, piercing stare. As his gaze centered on her mouth his eyes narrowed, the tiny lines fanning out to the sides, and she felt an excited shiver dance across her nerves.

Silently he took her hand, pulling her behind him, leading her into the confined space where several people were dancing.

Not a word was spoken between them, and yet their touch said everything. He wrapped his arms around her, and she felt a thrill of excitement shooting through her veins, the blood pounding in her pulse points. His touch opened something inside her, and she was offering herself, waiting for him to mold her as he wished. She felt exposed and invaded, as surely as if she were naked and pinned beneath his crushing weight, her flesh melting into his.

The music floated around her, and Kat sensed that they were moving to its rhythm. But the music could have stopped and she would not have known or cared. It was enough to be moving within the circle of Doug's arms, their bodies forming a rhythm of their own, their thighs touching and burning at the contact.

His lips brushed across her hair, resting momentarily at her ear before trailing down the side of her neck. The delicious scent of his after-shave mingled pleasurably with his own masculine smell, and Kat felt her heart pounding in response to the feel of him against her.

With her hand on the back of his head, Kat wound her fingers through the strands of Doug's brown hair, tugging at it involuntarily at the precise moment his hand moved across her hips, pressing her closer to him.

The slow music stopped, followed by a popular rock song that defied any attempts at close dancing. Moving away from the dance area, Doug leaned against the back of a couch and pulled Kat between the spread of his legs. Standing with her arms around his neck and his arms around her waist, Kat felt a baffling mixture of excitement and contentment, as if she and Doug had always been together as lovers and friends. She knew it was a strange way for her to feel in lieu of the fact that they had never really been either.

"What are you doing here?" His caressingly low voice rushed over her with velvet smoothness, sending tingling sensations skipping upward from the base of her spine.

"Prostitution." She had to fight for her breath.

"What!" His hands clenched her waist tightly, holding her at arm's length, and she saw the muscles of his jaw snap angrily.

Kat smiled wickedly at him, enjoying his moment of discomposure, before turning sober and explaining her situation. "I feel like I'm prostituting myself," she whispered, kneading Doug's neck until he relaxed his hold on her waist. "I wanted an interview—one of my editors is expecting an interview—with Sam Calhoun, and the only way he would give me one was if I came to this party." She glanced around hopelessly. "Although it doesn't look like I'm going to get one anyway."

"Disappointed?" Her gaze lifted from his chest to meet his eyes, and the unveiled look of inflamed desire she saw there left her knees weak. If it hadn't been for his arms around her waist, supporting her, she would have crumbled at his feet.

"No," she sighed. "Not disappointed." Never with you, she wanted to add.

Standing up, his eyes never leaving her face, he led her from the suite, past the dubious and curious stares of those who knew, or at least had read often enough, what Kat Ingles thought of Doug Hayden.

With his arm around her waist, they walked two doors down the hall to Doug's room. Pulling the key from his pocket, he watched her face, trying to read the play of emotions in her features, looking for some sign other than the one of uncertainty he saw.

"What are you thinking?" His hands pressed down on the tops of her shoulders, his head cocked slightly to one side.

"Oh, nothing, I was—" She was prepared to lie about her thoughts but stopped before the words were spoken. There had been too many lies between them. The time for truth was now. "I . . . was thinking about . . . about your wi—" The word stuck in her throat, the thought of him belonging—even in the past—to anyone else too painful to verbalize.

"My wife." His voice was flat and unemotional. He finished turning the key and pushed open the door. But he didn't enter. Instead, he leaned against the frame, staring into the room with almost vacant eyes. Suddenly, as she watched, a spark of fire flashed back into the blue depths, and he shifted his smoldering gaze toward her. "Katherine." He again grasped her shoulders. "Don't let it matter. Don't let my past mistakes come between us. Please." Their was a note of urgency in his voice, an undercurrent of need as desperate as her own.

She wouldn't let it matter. Nothing would matter but the fact that they—that *she* loved *him*. The revelation that she loved him struck her forcibly with its truth. She did love him! It wasn't just the physical longing for him. It was all of him: those laughing eyes and that winning smile; his easy wit and even temperament; his strong, athletic masculinity; and his boyish charm. It was him, pure and simple. All of the images that had haunted her waking and sleeping hours for so long melded into one Doug Hayden, each a part of, and inseparable from, the other.

Moving her hands up his chest, slowly, feeling his heart pounding, she laced her fingers around his neck. Smiling, opening herself to whatever he would give her, she breathed, "It doesn't matter, Doug. I promise."

Expelling the breath he had been holding for several long seconds while Kat's hands played across his chest, he pulled her inside, closing the door and leaning his weight against it. Folding her in the circle of his arms, his breath came quick and ragged against her ear.

For a few minutes they stayed that way, holding each other and feeling the warmth and security of their bodies so close. Pulling his head back to see her face, his gaze focused first on her love-filled eyes and then dropped to her parted, expectant lips.

His mouth moved across the surface of her lips, testing, softening, holding back.

"When I saw you with Calhoun this afternoon, I was like a mad dog." His voice was low against her mouth.

"If I had known you were going to be here at the party, I might not have come," she admitted softly.

"Then I would have had to wake you up in the middle of the night again. Only this time"—he smiled seductively—"you wouldn't have gotten rid of me so easily."

"I wouldn't even have tried."

Suddenly all teasing was gone. The need for her was too great. The pressure of his lips on hers increased, and his tongue plunged into her mouth, her own tongue meeting his in a sweeping blaze of desire. All the floodgates opened and the passion spilled over.

His hand grasped the back of her head, his fingers tangling in the thick mass of red hair. His other hand slid down her side, massaging her hip bone and pressing her into the hardened thrust of his body.

His mouth moved away from her lips, only to caress her face and neck and shoulders.

"How did I ever let you get away from me?"

His hand began unfastening the buttons on the front of her silk dress, impatiently pushing the material aside to allow his fingers the freedom they desired. His hand played across each of her breasts, stroking, caressing, his thumb and finger grasping her nipples, forming them into stiff peaks.

Unable to find the voice to answer his question, her own hand moved between their bodies, opening his shirt so her fingers could wind through the hair on his chest. Moving her hand down his stomach, past his belt buckle, down, she heard his sharp intake of breath. Lifting her suddenly in his arms, he carried her to the bed, where he followed her down to the mattress.

His mouth moved to her breasts, where his hands had been, and her fingers tugged at his soft brown hair, the gold highlights of which glowed softly in the dim light of the room.

While his lips and tongue stroked her nipples, his right hand completed the enjoyable task of undressing her, and she was pinned beneath him, naked, feeling the roughness of his pants between them. He grasped her hips, arching her toward him. For a few moments it was enough to rock and thrust gently against each other. But soon their needs became too great to delay.

As Doug rose reluctantly from the bed to pull his pants off, Kat stared, unable to take her eyes off his perfect frame. She had never seen a man like this before, and she knew that however frustrating the years of sexual innocence might have been, to be here now with Doug had been worth the wait.

Lowering himself to her, their eyes were locked in an embrace that ignited all time in one breathtaking, fiery moment. As their lips met so did their whole bodies.

There was an initial stabbing pain, and Kat grasped Doug's skin with her nails. She felt him stop, every muscle of his body tensed.

"Kather—" His breath was coming in short, sharp gasps. "God—why didn't you tell—" He knew, but he could not acknowledge it further. He couldn't wait; his needs were too strong now to stop and talk. But he stroked her slowly, gently, bringing her along with him.

She felt alive! Alive in a way she never dreamed possible. She was a part of him and he of her. Their bodies had melded into one, moving together. There was no pain now, only a building inside her, something growing and expanding until, grasping his back, their moans mingled together in the velvet softness of the night.

The light in the room seemed brighter than it had before, everything revealed in crystal clarity, a sharpness of focus that appeared more substantial than reality itself.

Doug rolled off her, his arm keeping her body next to his. Sliding her head onto his chest, she felt the circle of his arms closing around her, solid, his mouth touching her temple.

"Katherine, I had no idea." His breath fanned through her hair, the warmth of it touching her scalp. "You've never—" His voice was softly questioning, and she placed her fingers across his lips.

"I'm glad there's never been anyone else, Doug. You

were wonderful . . . and I want you to teach me everything. I want to make you feel as good as you make me feel. Don't feel sorry for me."

"Feel sorry for you!" He chuckled softly against her hair, then rolled over on top of her, pinning her expertly beneath him. She watched a seductive smile form on his lips, and the blue lights flared brilliantly in his eyes. "I'm not feeling sorry for you, honey. I'm counting my blessings.

"To know that you have given me . . . have shared with me . . . something that you've never shared with anyone else." His lips teased the corner of her mouth, his words coming between kisses. "No woman has ever shared that first time with me, Katherine. Not even my—no woman." His lips pressed against hers, molding hers to the shape of his, his tongue tracing their outline.

It was happening again, this wild, crazy tingling inside, in the deepest part of her. She wanted him again, and she could feel that he wanted her.

Doug's hands began their magic once more, and Kat felt all the long, lonely years melt away into one blissful rush of sensation.

CHAPTER SEVEN

The clarity of all things continued to astound her. Kat couldn't remember ever being able to see things as clearly as she now could. Especially Doug. She had never realized just how special he was. The man that the fans had loved for years was the man Kat now saw. She was held captive by his smile, a thrilling shiver of excitement passing through her every time he looked her way and grinned. He was hers. That was the most exciting part of all. The fans might adore him, follow his career with eager anticipation, praise and defend him, but Kat knew him. Only she could claim his love.

It was true, he had not yet said the words "I love you," but she knew he did just the same. It was written in the lines of his face, in the blue eyes that softened whenever they were focused on her.

To all appearances the tournament continued the next day as usual. Only Kat knew that nothing was as usual. Nothing would ever be the same again.

Doug lost his lead on Saturday and was then two strokes behind in the tournament. Two other players were tied at seven under, one stroke ahead of Doug, and, with only nine holes left to play in the match, Kat worried about whether he could handle the pressure on Sunday afternoon.

The total purse for the tournament was three hundred thousand dollars. If Doug won that day's round, he would walk away with over fifty thousand for the tournament. Last year he had been one of the top money winners, and so far this year, his winnings exceeded what they had been the previous year. With his endorsements and magazine advertisements, he would be earning an amount well into the six figures. However, the loss of several tournaments could set him back substantially. Sponsors were fickle, backing one player one month and a more promising newcomer the next. Unlike football or baseball players, who were paid salaries and travel expenses regardless of whether the team won a particular game or not, golfers' travel and equipment expenses were out of their own pockets, and their only salary came from their winnings. If a golfer had a bad day, he had no teammates to back him up. It was all up to him.

After the ninth hole Kat was hot and tired and needed something cold to drink. But she couldn't leave Doug. She was too tense about the outcome of each hole to miss even one. So, instead of heading for the clubhouse for a break, she followed the crowd over to the tenth tee, where a large gallery awaited Doug's foursome.

Doug was only a few feet away, with his back turned toward her. He was swinging his driver with his left hand, making large practice sweeps through the short-cropped grass. As if feeling the heat from her eyes on his back, he turned and smiled at her. She felt a shiver of delight rush through her only seconds before it was replaced by apprehension.

His smile faded quickly, and she watched him grow tense, the muscles of his body rigid, his mouth compressed into a tight, forbidding line. Kat frowned, not understanding what could have caused this strange shift in expression.

At that moment someone touched her shoulder. She turned to face a man she now recognized as one of the rookie golfers who had not made the cut in this tournament.

"Miss—Ingles?" The man's voice came in spurts between rasping breaths.

"Yes?" She was a little apprehensive over this man's obvious rush to speak to her. Was it an emergency of some sort? Her family! Was someone ill? Her eyes shifted back nervously to Doug, and she was startled by the fierce anger that was etched into his tanned features, the savage look that darkened his eyes with condemnation. Even at this distance, she could see the muscle that worked convulsively in his jaw. Was he looking at her? Or was he staring at the man who had just approached her?

She was confused as she watched the rookie golfer lift the bright-yellow golf hat from his head and, with a look of smug satisfaction and a wicked gleam in his eye, wave it at Doug.

Turning back to Kat, the man introduced himself. "I'm Jim Sanders, Miss Ingles."

"Yes, I know who you are. I've seen you play. You—" She was ready to make some trite remark about how his game was improving, when he interrupted her.

"Miss Ingles, I have to talk to you. It's"—he looked toward Doug—"very important."

Making note of the seriousness of Jim's tone of voice and expression, Kat nodded. "All right. Now?"

"Yes, now." He started to lead her away, but she stopped him. Doug had stepped up to the tee and was making his swing. Kat and those in the gallery watched the ball hook much too far to the left with an ominous crack, landing in the rough, well behind a large clump of pine trees.

Doug did not turn around again to look at Kat. He walked over to his golf bag, thrusting the club inside. With a blank expression, he watched the other players drive their balls expertly to the center of the fairway.

In the opposite direction of the moving crowd, Kat walked away with Jim Sanders.

He strode briskly, leading her toward the clubhouse. She grasped his elbow and tried to catch her breath. "Mr. Sanders—where are we going?"

"We need privacy." His features were set in unbending lines of determination, and Kat felt that, for now at least, she would not argue.

Finally stopping under the shade of a large blue spruce, Jim Sanders sat down. "Sit down, Miss—may I call you Kat?" There was not a friendly note in his voice.

Kat remained standing. "Uh—yes, but—Jim, if this is a social—I would like to get back to—" She pointed in the direction of the tenth green.

"This is not a social visit, Kat. And believe me, you will not consider it a waste of time."

Taking in the grim set of his mouth and jaw, Kat sat on the grass beside him.

"Okay, Jim, what's this all about?"

"It's about Doug Hayden." His eyes narrowed on her face, waiting for her reaction.

Trying to appear poker-faced, Kat responded with a meaningless "Oh."

"Listen." He leaned toward her conspiratorially. "I know what you think about Hayden—or at least what you thought in the past." His voice took on a note of accusation.

She started to comment, but he held up his hand to silence her. "Wait, let me finish. I have a story that no one else could cover as well as you. It's perfect for you. Or, I guess I should say you're perfect for *it.*" Jim plucked a clump of grass from the ground, shredding it nervously between his fingers. His eyes took on a feverish glow, and his mouth curled into an unfriendly smile. In sudden agitation he brushed his fingers against his pants, trying to remove the grass stains.

"Doug Hayden is winning tournaments . . . by cheating."

If Jim had slapped her in the face, Kat couldn't have been more startled. Shocked by such an outrageous idea, her mouth gaped wide, no sound pouring forth. She wanted to laugh at this ridiculous man with his preposterous allegation.

"That is ridiculous!" Though the words came out, the laugh remained stuck in her throat.

"Is it?" he sneered. "Have you watched him this last year? Have you seen how he so often comes from behind to win in the last three or four holes?"

"But—"

"Did you notice how he knocked his ball conveniently into the rough a minute ago? How he's now behind with only nine holes to play and how easy it will be for him to adjust his lie so that he has a perfect shot to the green?"

"Mr. Sanders, you are assuming that just because he had a bad shot on this last hole, that he would cheat to improve it?" Kat was incredulous.

"How do you think he has been able to win four of the last five tournaments, Kat?"

"My God!" she cried. "You're a golfer. You should know that everybody has good and bad times. That a golfer can have a streak of good luck, a whole series of wins! Don't be absurd! Doug is not the kind of man to cheat."

"There's more." His words were jerky and impatient, his cheek twitching nervously. "I heard him talking with some men. Not golfers . . . nasty little punks of some sort. It was agreed upon that Doug would do whatever he had to do to win. Doug agreed to do it, Kat," he emphasized, seeing her disbelieving stare.

"I can't believe that!" She wanted to tell this man to go straight to hell, but something about him, about his need for her to believe him, held her back. And suddenly she remembered seeing him in Florida. He was the man who had been standing in the gallery. The one Doug had stared at so intently. An ominous shudder rippled through her body.

"Why, for God's sake? What could possibly make him do that?"

"That's what you're to find out."

"Me!" She was stunned. "Who—why would I want to look into a preposterous allegation like that?" This was ridiculous! She didn't believe it in the first place, and she certainly wasn't going to waste her time following up a rumor like that. "I think you should know that my feelings about Doug have changed . . . we're—I—"

"I know exactly what's going on," he sneered contemptuously. "And if you'd use that pretty head of yours, you'd know, too."

"Just exactly what is that supposed to mean?" She did not like this smirking little man, and his superior attitude was starting to grate on her nerves.

"What that means is that Doug Hayden knows that I know about his . . . deal with those greasy hoods."

Kat's eyes stuck on his face, unmoving, afraid to hear what he might say next, yet knowing that, somehow, her ecstatic happiness of the past two days was about to crumble at her feet.

"And," Jim continued with a sick grin, "he knows how you feel—or felt—about him. I let him know that the public was going to find out about this. And he knew who I would come to with the story. All those other suckers who call themselves journalists . . . they're a bunch of leeches—parasites who cling to whoever is on top for the moment. Right now they're blind to his faults, but once the story is out, they'll jump on the bandwagon, too. But you"—his eyes drilled through the center of her head—"you are better than they are. You have always written it like it is. You were the one person who could see through that putrid boy scout routine of his."

The ferocious bitterness pinched his face into ugly lines, and his voice had a flat, nasal quality. "I knew you were the only one who would find the truth and print it. Hayden knew that, too. He knows that the rest of the pack are spineless idiots. But you—he could be pretty sure that if you believed it, you'd write about it. Why in the hell do you think he's pounced on you like a chicken on a junebug?"

Kat gasped. "How dare—" The thought that he had been watching them was disconcerting enough. But to hear his insinuations about Doug's motives was intolerable.

"I dare because I know," he snarled. "I dare because it's true. I've been watching Hayden for a long time, sister, and I know all of his tricks. You think you're the first woman who's been caught in his clutches? Well, you're not! No, they all fall for him . . . just like you." His eyes had taken on a glazed look, a faraway stare that frightened and sickened Kat. "He's used you, Kat Ingles. He got to you, hoping to sway you to his side so you wouldn't listen to me. 'Cause he knew I would come to you. If you can't see that, you're not only blind, you're stupid."

Kat's eyes swung away from Jim, then back to his face, her features pulled tight in an expression of anguish. She couldn't speak! She couldn't think! She had to get away from this man!

As though he were reading her thoughts, he grasped her arm. "Before you run away you'd better know that the editor at *Golfer's Monthly* believes what I've told him."

Kat's eyes narrowed in disbelief.

"At least he believes it enough to have it looked into. I told him you would be the one."

"You had no right to do that!" she hissed.

"I had every right," he barked. "I want Hayden off the Tour, and believe me, I'll do everything in my power to get him ousted. So, I suggest that if you want to retain your somewhat dubious relationship with that editor, you'd better give him a call. Otherwise, I would be willing to guess you can kiss your career good-bye."

Emotionally unable to think about herself and what this meant to her, Kat concentrated on the distorted face of Jim Sanders. "Why do you hate him so?" Her voice was flat and almost childlike.

"Like I said, you're not the first to fall into Hayden's clutches. He doesn't feel like a man unless he's stealing somebody else's woman. I learned that the hard way, and I've sworn ever since that Doug Hayden would pay for it. So, if you don't print this story, Miss Ingles, I will stop at nothing to make sure that the story is out and—and let it be known that you had a part in covering it up."

Kat stood up abruptly, unable to bear the sight of this perverted man anymore. Glaring at his self-satisfied smirk, she shoved her hands into the pockets of her jeans.

"You're a bastard, Mr. Sanders."

Her head was pounding, the pain reverberating between her temples. It couldn't be true! It couldn't! Doug wouldn't do such a thing. He wouldn't have done that to her. She gave him everything she had to give. She trusted him! She shared with him her most precious gift—her love.

God, please don't let this be happening! Please let it all be a dream. She would wake up from this nightmare, catch up with Doug and his foursome, and the pain would be gone. Doug would be smiling at her, his love as real as she believed it to be.

The afternoon was dragging by almost interminably. By the time Kat got up the nerve to face Doug, he and his foursome were already on the sixteenth hole. She approached the green slowly, moving inconspicuously among the throng of people in the gallery.

She had to force herself to look at the cards being carried by the scorekeeper. She didn't want to know. But she looked. Oh, damn! He was six under par, and in second place. It's a coincidence that he has come from behind to win the last few tournaments! It has to be. After all, he's a great player. He wouldn't cheat to win. He could win on his own skill! Surely he doesn't need the fifty thousand dollars badly enough to cheat. Does he? There would be no reason for him to do that.

Her mind was raking through the possibilities when she

looked up. There he was, standing in the sand trap on the opposite side of the green, his pitching wedge lofting the ball onto the green within eight feet of the cup.

His gaze followed the ball, then lifted to the crowd beyond. He saw her, and his face locked in an unreadable expression. His eyes bored through her, examining, looking into that bottomless pit of her thoughts. His jaw was clenched shut, his mouth a grim, tight line.

Kat didn't move, she couldn't. The muscles of her face were frozen into a mask of uncertainty, an unwillingness to believe the lies, and yet a fear—a terrible, cold fear—that what Jim Sanders had said was true.

The deadlock was broken when Doug walked onto the green to place a marker under his ball so that the other players could putt. He did not look at her again.

When it was his turn to putt, he walked to the marker, replaced it with his ball, centered his body over the ball, and pulled his putter back and through, pushing it toward the cup. The ball swerved slightly, avoiding the hole by a slim margin. The groans in the crowd echoed against the uncertain canyons of Kat's mind.

He should have made that! He shouldn't have missed that putt! Now, if he were to win the lead, he might have to—to cheat! Glancing at Doug's face, the smug set of his features was the last expression Kat expected to see. Is he admitting it? Is that what he's saying? Look, Katherine, you sucker, see what I'm doing? Now, tell me if you're going to do something about it. He was daring her! That's what she read in his face, because that's what he was saying.

A huge lump of nausea rising in her throat, Kat turned and pushed frantically through the gallery, running toward the clubhouse.

Approaching it in a state of near panic, she rushed for the press tent, shoving her way through curious onlookers, heading blindly for the telephone. Grasping the receiver, she paused, not sure she should even make the call. But remembering the arrogant look of daring on Doug's face triggered her reaction, and she dialed the New York number she had memorized so long ago.

Just after dusk large cumulus clouds grew tall and dark in the sky, their tops flattened like anvils. Distant and intermittent thunder volleyed across the western sky, and the line between the darkening sky and the tops of the green pine trees became almost imperceptible.

For a while Kat watched the clouds building in the sky from behind the windows of her van. The threatening noise of the approaching rainstorm compounded the revolving storm of emotions that was lashing at her mind from all directions. But then she sat on the couch at the back of the van, staring at the bottom of the empty glass on the table. She had been sitting that way for an hour, her mind unwilling to think or to make her body move. It was too much to comprehend, too much to accept.

The only man in the whole world she had ever loved was Doug. And now, as if the devil of her fantasies had, in actuality, been transformed into a nightmarish reality, she was faced with a torture far surpassing that in any of her dreams.

Her hands were clasped tightly around the glass, tipping it slightly toward her so that she had a better view of the interior. It was as if she were looking inside herself, inside her soul. Barren, colorless, evaporated. They were one and the same, this glass and she. They were both glass shells, containing nothing of substance inside, only a hollow emptiness.

It had begun raining, but the sound of the splattering drops did not penetrate the thick fog shrouding Kat's mind. A knock on the door finally roused her out of her gloomy reverie. She stared at the closed metal door as if she had never seen the thing before, as if she had never heard the sound of a fist against metal. The knock came again, more insistent and louder this time.

"Go away," she muttered. She didn't want to see anyone.

"Open up, Katherine." The voice was as loud and insistent as the knocking had been.

Oh, God, what did he want? "Go away," she repeated, louder this time.

"Katherine, you either open this goddamn door, or I swear I'll break it down!" She heard that note in his voice, that inflection that made her pay attention. She knew he meant what he was saying. He would break it down.

Forcing her legs to support her weight, she stood, feeling old and infirm. Walking on leaden feet to the door, she swung it open, letting it slam against the outside of the van.

He was dressed as he had been that afternoon, his knit shirt now clinging wetly to his chest, drops of water dripping from his hair down his face. Staring at her ghostly pale face for a long, penetrating moment, Doug stepped up into the van, brushing Kat aside as he closed the door.

Kat leaned against the counter, her hands grasping the edge for support. It was an emotional and physical crutch, and right then she needed all the help she could get.

Doug stuffed his hands in his pockets, his stance tense and on guard. His face was pulled together in a frown, his eyebrows lowered, his jaw hard and unyielding, his lips tight and forbidding. "What are you going to do, Katherine?"

She listened carefully to his tone of voice. There was no note of pleading, no dare, no threat. Nothing. There was nothing in his voice. It was flat and unemotional. Each word was uttered distinctly and slowly, and her mind reeled with the message he was trying to transmit but that she could not read. He hadn't wasted time asking her what Jim Sanders was talking to her about. He knew, and that fact alone weighed heavily on Kat's decision.

There was no denying the accusation, no explanation. He wanted merely to know what she was going to do about it. But, God, what *was* she going to do about it?

"My editor—" She cleared her throat and began again. "My editor thinks you're—he went over the records of your past six months. He—he wants me to—to look into it."

"And you always do what you're told, don't you, Katherine?" His voice was bitter now, scathing and harsh, and she felt his scorn penetrate her last fortification.

"Deny it!" she yelled, tears pushing their way to the front of her eyes. "Deny it, damn it!" She slammed her fist onto the counter, sending a knife bouncing across the surface. "It's my job, Doug! I'm a reporter! If it's not true, deny it!" Tears were rolling down her cheeks now, and she brushed at them impatiently with the back of her hand.

Doug lifted his right hand from his pocket, reaching out to grasp her chin gently between his fingers. Leaning closer, his head lowered toward her face, his mouth stopping within inches of her lips. Her breathing stopped, a rippling wave of heat crashing in upon her. That mouth! To taste those lips again.

She could feel his breath warm and soft on her lips, could smell the intoxicating maleness of his sweat, and she could feel the electrical impulses from his mouth. His mouth was almost touching hers . . .

"Enjoy your career, Katherine."

As Doug pulled away abruptly from Kat the cold glare from his eyes immediately froze the current that had been running like fire through her body. She was devastated.

With numbed senses, she watched him open the door and look back at her one more time with that same unfathomable gaze, then step down onto the ground, closing the door behind him.

With the final click of the closing door, Kat felt something close inside her. It was as if at the same moment someone latched the door to her soul, where nothing would enter and nothing would leave.

She began laughing, uncontrollable, hysterical laughter that soon became a torrent of tears and racking sobs.

CHAPTER EIGHT

October was ignited in all its blazing glory, exploding with radiant color and cool, stimulating temperatures. Even with the decline of summer, nature still gave bountifully of its beauty, the brilliant colors representing the zenith of the year's cycles. Like the setting of the sun, the colors of fall deepen and glow, then gradually grow darker and duller until the season drops over the rim into winter.

Kat had forgotten how beautiful the fall could be in the Midwest. The dogwoods, elms, and maples were bursting with color, their leaves like flames leaping up the trunks of the trees.

Kat had returned to Kansas City three weeks earlier to her parents' house and to what she hoped would be neutral territory where she could decide rationally what must be done.

The belief that Doug had used her and her love for him to buy her silence filled her with almost unbearable emotional pain. And she was angry—with him for his calculating moves, and with herself for playing the fool. Her thoughts floated vaguely somewhere between the desire for revenge and the desire for the physical release that could come only through forgiveness of him.

Her mental reflections had been tested to the limit these weeks, and still she had come to no definite decisions concerning Doug. But she had decided one thing for sure. There was absolutely nothing glorious in loneliness, no splendor in defeat. No rewards in hard times, that she could see.

She had been anxious to return home, back to the breast where she could be protected from the cruelty of adulthood. She wasn't at all sure she liked being a woman. She assumed that once she was with her parents again, she would find the answers she needed. She would be buffered against more hurt, and they would decide for her on her course of action. She assumed wrong.

Kat went home, but things were not the same. Furniture had been rearranged, and the chair in which she used to sit in comfort was gone. She realized that it was, of course, more than that. Her parents' life had gone on without her. She was a grown woman, and through her own choice had pushed herself out of the womb. Now she would have to solve her own problems.

Yet, she still had to admit that her father had been a great comfort to her. She had related to him enough of the story, without adding the personal details, so that he knew what was troubling her. But she had never been able to conceal much from him. He knew. He knew from the way in which her green eyes darkened to the color of shaded moss when she spoke of Doug. He knew from the exaggerated upward tilt of her head, which masked the pain she felt inside. He knew and he understood the private war that was waging in her mind. She had a hard choice to make. She could close her mind to the possibility that Doug was doing something wrong, letting love divert her from her own hopes and aspirations for a career as a writer. Or she could search out the facts, learn the truth, and accept whatever she found. It would not be an easy decision for his strong-willed daughter, but she would pull through it. She was too much like him to let it keep her incapacitated for long.

He was right. By the end of the third week at home, she was ready to tackle the problem. She would start here in Kansas City. After all, it was where Doug had been brought up, where he had first begun his golf career. It was his proving ground as an amateur golfer.

But how in heaven's name was she going to be able to find proof for such an allegation! It was still so absurdly unbelievable. Golfers just didn't do that sort of thing. This wasn't horse racing, where off-track-betting encouraged illicit activities. This was golf. The gentleman's sport for the Jack Daniel's and Cadillac set. And Doug—the all-American male, clean-cut, witty, charming—was hardly the criminal type.

Still, she had been given certain allegations that she couldn't ignore. He had been seen and heard making a deal with—what had Jim Sanders called them—greasy hoods? And he had won four of the last five tournaments in the last nine holes. Of course, that could have been due to other forces, like skill or luck. But still, she had to take it into account.

Also, the editor of *Golfer's Monthly* thought there was enough evidence to at least check it out. He reminded Kat of the case a few years ago of a woman golfer who was caught changing her ball marker on the greens. But that woman was found out, and if Doug was cheating, surely he realized he would be caught before long.

But the most disturbing fact of all, and the one Kat had the most trouble dealing with, was Doug's sudden interest in her after so many years. Why had he pursued her out of the blue? It was true that in the past she had avoided him. Still, if he had wanted her, he could have had her. But no, it only happened recently, after Jim had made his knowledge known to Doug. He had pursued Kat and, using all of his masculine charms, had pinned her beneath him, both physically and emotionally.

He had made sure he covered every angle. Even that night at Sam Calhoun's party, he had merely been staging a show for all to see. By making it obvious to everyone there that he and Kat had a relationship, he was insuring their loyalty. Everyone would assume naturally that anything Kat wrote about Doug would have a totally unobjective viewpoint.

However, Kat tried to push aside her emotional feelings as she delved into Doug's past. She began by researching the records of his wins and losses on the amateur circuit but could come up with nothing that appeared suspicious. He had won some and lost some, but there appeared to be no pattern to his wins. His reputation with golf instructors and other golfers was impeccable. In school, he had been a bright student who caused mischief now and then, but who never was anything but honest and hardworking. Nothing in Doug's past pointed to dishonesty. He was the farthest thing from a cheat.

Finally deciding there was nothing left for her to do in Kansas City, Kat said good-bye to her parents, moved herself and Bogie back into the van, and headed east across Missouri, where the next tournament would begin on Thursday.

The golf course and country club lay amidst the rolling hills of one of the poshest suburbs of St. Louis. It was an older, established club, and the trees that lined the fairways were large and gnarled. But their leaves were bold with the colors of autumn, and they provided a startling contrast to the lush, lingering green of the fairways.

Kat arrived on Thursday, the first day of the Bridge Forest Open. A hundred and fifty players were to be competing not only to make the cut, but to assume the lead. Eighteen holes would be played that day and eighteen on Friday, and by then the officials would have determined the sixty or so players who would make the cut and compete in the next thirty-six holes.

It was overcast when Kat arrived, and the sky threatened rain before the day was out. Kat parked her van in the lot and slapped her parking sticker on the inside of the windshield. This time she had remembered to send off for her credentials and wouldn't have to undergo the scrutiny of the tournament officials to receive her badge.

Leaving the windows open only a crack for Bogie, in case it rained, Kat walked toward the press tent, slinging her tote bag over her shoulder.

The air was solid with the chill of fall, and she was glad she had thought to bring a cardigan sweater along. Though she felt haggard from the strain she had been under the past few weeks, those who laid eyes on her saw only a beautiful redhead dressed in perfectly fitting designer jeans, a soft green jersey T-shirt that matched the color of her eyes, and a navy sweater tied by the sleeves around her shoulders, and who had a determined stride that reflected the resoluteness of her character.

Picking up her badge in the tent, she was overjoyed when she spotted Tim at a table along the edge. She rushed over to the table and threw her arms around his back and shoulders.

"Oh, Tim," she cried. "It's so good to see you. I can't even tell you how good."

"Hi, Kat." He squeezed her arms. "Things have been that bad, huh?" he teased, but Kat detected a trace of malice that she had never noticed in Tim before. Despite his affectionate overtures something was different about him.

Warily nodding her head to answer his correct assumption, she sat down next to him at the table, glad to have his company but worried about what might be bothering him.

He was sitting by himself, making notes in a notebook, and Kat got a Coke from the ice box while he finished. Sipping her drink, she smiled and tried to make conversation. Tiring quickly of simple chitchat, she leaned back in her chair and sighed.

"How could I have ever thought this would be a glamorous profession?" She looked around the open-air room. "Just look at this group," she said with disgust. "Sometimes I think I have no business being here."

"You're probably right, Kat." Tim was staring into his drink, his lips pursed derisively. "You should be home somewhere, pleasing a man and keeping fat with his babies."

If anything could have startled her out of her gloomy despondency, it was a remark like that. Kat glowered at Tim as if he had lost his mind. He raised his eyebrows and shrugged his shoulders.

"Is that what you wanted to hear?"

"Damn it, Tim! You know that's not what I meant. It's just that—"

"You love him, don't you?"

"What!" She turned round eyes upon him. "What are you blabbering about?" she whispered.

"Doug Hayden. That's what all this soul-searching is about, isn't it?"

"Whatever gave you that idea?" She feigned nonchalance, but she could tell Tim wasn't fooled.

"I thought we were better friends than that, Kat." He seemed hurt, disappointed in her, and she dropped her gaze to stare dejectedly at her Coke can.

"Tim, it's such a long story. It's not simply a matter of—"

"I know about the article you're working on." She jumped in her seat, turning startled green eyes on him. "And I'm not the only one."

"How did you find out? Who told you?" she whispered anxiously.

"I don't even remember now, Kat. But it's leaking out fast, and the fans are starting to get wind of something foul in the air, too." His voice had taken on a hard edge, and she could tell he was angry.

"You don't believe it, do you, Tim?" She wanted him to say no, wanted to have someone tell her it wasn't true.

"No, I don't." A flash of anger darted across his eyes, and his mouth stretched thin and tight. It was the first time Kat had ever seen him this way. "You realize, if it's not true, you could be ruining the man's career."

"And if it is true?" Her voice sliced the air sharply. He had no right to lay blame on her for ruining Doug's career. She hadn't started any rumors.

"You don't believe he's guilty any more than I do." Tim stared at her with a faintly disgusted look.

There was a long pause when neither of them spoke. She had angered her best friend *and* betrayed the man she loved. What must Tim think of her!

"You act as though you love him," he continued. "But

maybe you've just used him to get a story. Which is it? Are you desperate for an exclusive story or a physical relationship? Is Hayden just another body to you? Or is he your means to 'the Great American Exposé'?"

She was too stunned to answer. His rapid-fire questions had left her bewildered and hurt.

"Well, if that's what it is . . . Damn!" Tim rose to leave, then, on second thought, turned back suddenly and leaned over her chair. "I just hope to hell you find it all worth it, Kat." With angry strides Tim shoved through the crowd and out into the muted fall day.

It was several agonizing minutes before Kat could move. She raised her head and stared outside, where the overhanging clouds looked thick and darkening. A brown, curling leaf dropped from a tree branch, falling onto a small pile of others that were making way for new life to form.

Tim was her best friend. How could he think such a thing about her? She used Doug? Didn't he realize it was the other way around? Doug was the one who used *her* to protect his own interests. Just a physical relationship to her? . . . She loved him! She loved him, and she didn't know what she was going to do!

The story was indeed out. And every time Kat overheard a comment from the gallery, berating Doug's perfect shots and attributing his excellent playing to the rumor, something in Kat's heart constricted. Had she done this? Was she to blame for the snide remarks she heard?

She hadn't let the story leak. That bastard, Jim Sanders, must have done it. He wasn't happy enough with the fact that Kat was going to look into it. No, he had to spread the vicious rumors around, assuring himself that Doug's career would crash around him. Essentially Kat had done nothing to harm Doug, and yet she felt as if she had inflicted a wound as surely as if she had thrust a poisoned dagger into his unsuspecting back.

It first hit her that it all was having a terrible effect on Doug when she saw him on the tenth green. She was waiting there, watching each foursome that came through, keeping a running tally of the scores and the way each golfer was playing in the first round.

When Doug's foursome approached the green she was stunned. His appearance had changed so drastically since she had seen him a month earlier. There were dark hollows under each eye, the blue of them muted and dull. But there was also a fleeting look of—was it panic? His features were drawn and tight, his mouth forcing a grin that may have fooled some of the fans, but Kat knew it was not the easy smile that belonged to the naturally happy Doug Hayden.

She watched him toss a joke to some people to his left, but when he turned back away from them, she could see the tension and defeat in his eyes, and he rubbed with his hand at a stiffness in his neck.

She recalled his words: "Why shouldn't I enjoy the role while it lasts? I'm not foolish enough to believe it will last forever. . . ." He hadn't realized how swiftly the pedestal of fame could be ripped from underneath him. *Dear God, what have I done to him!*

As she watched him putt Kat felt an unwanted heat building up inside her. Despite his tense, drawn appearance he still withdrew something from her that left her weak with desire. She had an almost uncontrollable urge to run through the gallery to him, to throw herself against him, dragging from him all the passion he could give her. In her mind she could see him reaching for her, pulling her into the fold of his sweat-covered arms, dragging her to the ground and covering her slighter frame with his heavier one, his lips searing into her flesh. In her fantasy the crowd would simply move on, leaving them alone in the soft grass to drive each other over the edge of desire, Doug taking her until he had had his fill.

She was startled to find that by the time she had shaken the fantasy from her mind, the foursome had moved to the eleventh tee and a new group was approaching the tenth green. Blushing hotly from her thoughts, she glanced nervously about, hoping no one had been able to surmise the scene that had been enacted in her mind.

By the end of the day Doug was among the top five players in the tournament, and if he continued to play as well the next day, he would at least make the cut. The fact that he was playing well was the only relief Kat had from the guilt that tormented her.

She knew he wasn't guilty of cheating. She had convinced herself it wasn't true. She loved him, regardless of whether he loved her or not. He had used her, but it didn't matter. She knew now that she would be willing to do anything to be with him, even if it meant humiliating herself. To hell with her pride! She would take whatever small crumbs he tossed her way. As long as she could have a part of him, however small it might be.

As soon as the last foursome played the eighteenth green, Kat left with a subdued, but polite, Tim and a few other journalists to go to a pizza parlor near the club. She wanted to leave the restaurant early, but the men insisted on guzzling one pitcher of beer after another, and since she didn't have her own transportation there, she could do nothing but wait it out until they dropped her off in the club's parking lot around ten o'clock.

It had been a long, emotionally tense day, and Kat wanted nothing more than to go back to her van, take a shower, and crawl into bed. She would need her strength for the next day.

As she turned the key in the lock and opened the door of the van, Kat felt her skin tingle from the vague awareness of a presence beside her. Looking around cautiously, she stared into Doug's face.

Leaning his shoulder against the van, his body was tense, his eyes set and cold, a muscle working convulsively in his hard jaw.

Her hand froze on the door, her body unable to move either toward him or up into the van. She tried to swallow, but something was stuck in her throat.

When he spoke his voice was cold and hard. "Too bad you lost your exclusive rights to the story . . . now that the whole goddamn world knows." When his mouth clamped shut the twitch in his jaw began again.

Through the flood of desire that she felt for him, a surge of anger burst forth. "Exclusive—exclusive!" she stammered. "Is that what you think this is all about? You think I wanted the job of writing something that could destroy you?" Her blood was boiling, and she wanted to strike out at him, blindly, hurting him the way his words had hurt her.

"Well, you certainly don't seem to be too upset by it," he sneered. "Did you have fun with all your buddies tonight? What do you do, provide their entertainment when they're on the road, away from their wives?"

At the stinging affront she raised her hand, swinging it

back to gain the force needed to slap his cheek. Before her hand could touch flesh it was grasped in a grip of iron. The blaze in his molten hot eyes burned through her, igniting her, making her previous anger appear as nothing more than a slight upset.

Fiercely she fought him, trying to pull her hand away from his grip. With superhuman strength he forced her into the van, following her inside, never letting go of the wrist he was clamping. She felt no pain, for he had done nothing to hurt her physically. And yet she knew that she could not get away from him until he decided it was time. With this realization her fight subsided, hoping that perhaps with calm reasoning he would let her go.

Thinking otherwise, Doug twisted his left arm around her waist, trapping her against his hard body. His mouth came down demandingly on her parted lips, his anger reflected in the cruel pressure of his lips on hers. Her breasts were flattened against the wall of his chest, and she could smell the sweat of the day on him.

Letting go of her wrist, he circled her body with his other arm, lifting her in the tight band of his arms, carrying her twisting body to the bed at the back of the van. She hadn't folded it up into a couch this morning, and though she now cursed herself for being such a fool, it was too late to do anything about it.

As Doug fell down heavily on top of her, Kat continued to fight, but as the pressure on her mouth changed to passionate demand and his hands began to roam with fiery possessiveness over her hips and thighs, she felt her body slacken. It was what she wanted after all. God knew it was what she wanted! It was the spark of fire that burned through the fabric of her desires. With almost frantic movements she circled his neck with her arms, seizing a handful of his hair and pulling hard, wanting to hurt without hurting. Wanting to take all of what was him away from his body and put it into hers.

Sensing her acquiescence, Doug began moving his mouth across her face and neck, pulling her jersey T-shirt and her bra up until her breasts were bare before him. His mouth covered one of the firm mounds, his tongue rubbing hard across the nipple.

Moving back to her lips, his mouth once again invaded the receptive parted lips, his tongue plunging deeply inside to be met by hers, eagerly rough in response.

There was nothing gentle in his lovemaking, nothing pure and soft. It was a physical purging, a need that went beyond all other bounds. She felt it as strongly as he did. She needed him. She wanted him. And they would both drag it forcefully from each other.

Pulling back from her abruptly, Doug began removing his clothes. Kat sat up quickly and did the same. Their eyes never left each other's body, and she watched his breath coming in ragged pants, Doug reminding her of a fierce lion about to pounce hungrily on his intended prey.

Once they were undressed and their bodies were entwined again, their lovemaking continued its ferocious climb. She could feel the sweat still clinging to his back and neck, smell the drugging masculinity of him. She could grasp the muscles of his back and know the substance of him. It was a tangible thing; something she could sink her teeth into.

Their lovemaking was a tumultuous ascent that carried them higher and higher, to the brink of a steep precipice, suddenly throwing them over the edge, where they catapulted to the fiery depths below.

It was a very long time before either of them moved.

The weight of Doug's body was heavy upon Kat's, but she couldn't let go, didn't want to lose that solid reality that had once again become a part of her.

After awhile Doug raised himself on his elbows, taking most of the weight from her. Looking down, his eyes had lost the look of panic that she had noticed earlier and wondered about. But in its place was an intensity that left her weak with fright and desire. He wanted her again. And she would let him. She wanted him to want her again.

Moving her hands down the sweat-glistened wall of his chest and down his stomach, she could feel the muscles tightening in his abdomen. She made clear her own desires, and he hesitated for only a moment. His voice was hoarse and low.

"This time, I want you to talk to me." Then he hesitated no longer.

When Kat awoke she felt something heavy on her body. Trying without success to move it from her, she turned and was startled to find Doug next to her. It had really happened! It hadn't been another fantasy, another dream. He had been here with her.

His arm was draped possessively over her chest, and one knee was resting over her thigh. She relaxed, smiling to herself, and let the sleep drain slowly from her.

The tournament! She sat up, the sudden movement throwing his arm and leg off of her and jerking him awake.

"Doug! The tournament!"

"What time is it?" He jumped groggily from the bed, grabbing his pants from the pile of clothing that was thrown on the floor.

Kat threw the clothes on the floor to the side, grabbing

her clock, which had been underneath them. She pressed it to her ear to make sure it was still ticking, then sighed with relief. "It's seven. You've still got an hour."

Breathing deeply, Doug sat on the side of the bed, staring numbly at the rumpled shirt in his hands. "Hell, maybe it would be just as well if I had slept through the rounds today."

Shocked at his defeatist attitude, Kat cried, "No, Doug! You can't possibly believe that!"

He turned his head sharply to look at her, and the accusing stare that bore through her froze the blood in her veins.

Nothing had changed! Last night they had been receptacles for their anger, for their driving physical need for each other. They had solved nothing. The doubt still hung like a heavy tarp between them, letting nothing reach through but the physical connection.

She had to tell him she believed in him. She had to let him know that she loved him. Her hand rose as if she were about to reach out and touch his tan shoulder. She hesitated, stopping in midair. Facing facts, Kat couldn't bear the humiliation of having him laugh at her and reject her love. The day before, she had thought that she would suffer anything to be a part of his life, but something still held her back.

He had never said he loved her. And why should he? Why would he love someone who didn't believe in him, who doubted his honesty and integrity? No, he had never said that he loved her. But then, he had never even denied the rumors about himself either.

To all outward appearances Kat was a courageous woman, out on her own, following the golf tour in a live-in van, with nothing but a cat for companionship. But Kat knew better. She was a chicken. She didn't have the guts to put her heart on the line, with the chance of seeing it ripped loose in the wind. She was scared to death!

The hesitation of her hand in midair said it all.

CHAPTER NINE

The fair weather continued on Friday without a flaw. The sun's powerful rays were undaunted by the few wispy stratus clouds that trailed across the blue sky.

Doug's golf game continued without a flaw also. He couldn't do anything wrong. Every shot landed exactly where he had intended it to land, and, at ten under par, he now led the tournament by three strokes.

By the end of the day he still carried the lead, and the sixty players within ten strokes of his score all made the cut for the tournament. Saturday's and Sunday's results would determine the winner who would take home sixty thousand dollars.

All day Kat wondered at Doug's inner source of strength. The rumors about him were rampant, yet somehow he managed to keep a sense of humor and retain the powers of concentration needed for each shot.

Kat only wished she could have handled things half as well. Every time she heard a derogatory comment about Doug, every time someone berated his score with innuendos of his cheating, she would cringe inside. She was angry with anyone who would believe such vicious rumors and lies . . . and yet, she reminded herself, she was the one who had been the first to believe them.

Throughout the day her thoughts kept reverting to the night before, when Doug had come to her van. They had needed each other so desperately, had clung to the physical bond between them as if it were the last hold they would have on each other. If only she had told him she loved him. If only he had whispered some endearment to her. If only her pride and his reticence weren't hanging between them. If only . . . if only . . .

As the final foursome completed the eighteenth hole, Kat headed straight for her van, bypassing the press tent. She still wasn't quite used to the cold shoulder she had been receiving lately from the journalist fans of Doug Hayden. Tim was right. Everyone knew she was working on an article about Doug's alleged cheating, and most of them found the idea disgusting. Hayden would never stoop to something that low. In their minds, only a half-witted female reporter who desperately needed a boost to her career would dig up such smut as that.

Rather than subject herself to the hateful glares and contemptuous comments, Kat would not take a chance by entering the press tent. Besides, she preferred to do her typing in the privacy of her van, away from the distracting clang of numerous other typewriters.

Walking through the crowded parking lot, she had to squeeze between closely parked cars to make her way to the van.

As she rounded the bumper of a blue Ford sedan, she stopped in her tracks. Two men, dressed in faded jeans and well-worn cotton shirts, their hair slicked back in the style of the fifties, stood a few feet in front of her, the intensity of their glares threatening and ominous.

Kat stood still and stared, her eyes warily taking in their dress and processing the fact that they did not appear to belong at the golf tournament or in the plush country-club setting. Both men stared back at her, one with a leer that twisted his mouth to the side grotesquely, and the other with lips held so thin and tight, they almost seemed to disappear.

Her mind began racing to form a plan of escape. She wasn't sure what these creeps had in mind, but she certainly wasn't going to stand around and find out. The cars in the parking lot were so tightly packed together that she would have to squeeze through to get away. That would be too slow. They could catch up with her that way. But what else was there?

As if they knew she was ready to run, they moved toward her cautiously. Knowing that if she was going to get away, it would have to be then, she pivoted sharply and dashed back around the blue Ford, her tote bag slamming into the side of a car as she ran.

The two men had split up, one following behind her, and the other moving around in a circle to head her off. She was beginning to panic. She gasped for breath as she ran and looked around for someone to help her. Surely there was someone in the parking lot who could see that she needed help! Someone, please! She had heard so many stories of women being raped or murdered in broad daylight in a crowded area and no one helping the victim. But it wouldn't—it couldn't—be happening to her. No! She wouldn't let it.

With a snarl, she turned to glare at the two men stalking her, backing up slowly as she watched them. A courageous front was what she needed, she decided. They expected her to be frightened. But if she confronted them bravely, maybe they'd leave her alone. It was worth a try.

"What do you want?" she hissed, her claws bared for

an attack upon their flesh if it was necessary. They continued to stalk ever closer. "What do you want!" she cried. "Look, if it's money, I don't have any in my purse, but—but I could—get you some—I could find some for you." Finally accepting the fact that reasoning with them was going to get her nowhere, Kat took off running again. She realized then that she had been running away from the course and was closer to her van than to the crowd of golf spectators. She would have to try to make it there before they did.

As she ran she tried frantically to reach for her keys in the bottom of her tote bag, but they continued to elude the grasp of her hands, and the search only slowed her progress. She was sweating profusely, droplets of water running down her neck and chest. Her lungs felt as if they would explode from lack of air any minute.

Glancing over her shoulder to see where her pursuers were, she was startled to find that they had disappeared. Had she shaken their trail? She had been running fast, but they had been right behind her! Stopping long enough to grasp her keys, she headed quickly for her van. She was only a few cars away, and she had to get there before they picked up her trail again.

Stepping stealthily to the door, her hands shook as she tried to slip the key into the lock. It wouldn't fit! She tried again! And again! It took several tries before her shaking fingers could fit it into the space in the door. With a feeling of immense relief, she felt and heard the lock click. But her moment of reprieve was short-lived.

A large, dark hand clamped down over hers, gripping painfully both her fingers and the key she held in the door. As she turned to stare at the man beside her, a cold sweat broke out anew over her body. It was the one with the sick leer who held her hand. Turning her head the other way, Kat noticed the more serious man glaring at her. Her heart was pounding, and she felt the beads of sweat running down her face from her temples.

"What do you want?" Her voice was hoarse with fatigue and fear, and she tried to repeat the question. "What—"

"Shut up, Miss Ingles." It was the man to her left, with the tight mouth, who spoke. "Or you're gonna be hurt."

To emphasize that point the leering man squeezed her hand more tightly, the key pushing painfully into the bones of her fingers.

"Now, you listen real careful to what we got to say." The one on her left was speaking again, and Kat decided if she was to reason with one of them, it would probably be him. "You listen up good, 'cause I know you don't wanna get yourself messed up none. And, ya see, Matt here don't have much control when it comes to fine-lookin' broads like yourself." She stared with wide, frightened eyes at the man until she felt the other's hand placed at the small of her back. She swung to look at the leering one and paled as she realized how little she could do to stop these men from doing whatever they intended to do.

She turned back to the thin-mouthed man when she heard his voice again.

"I'm gonna tell you this just once. Stay away from that story you're writing about Doug Hayden."

Kat's mind reeled with the statement. It wasn't her they wanted! It was something to do with Doug!

"You drop it. You got that?"

She stared at him blankly, the message not transmitting to her confused mind.

"I don't think she understands, Matt." With painful

swiftness the one called Matt grabbed a handful of hair, pulling her head back to where her vision was filled with his leering face. He yanked her around until her back was against the van, her hand still grasped the key tightly. Tears sprang to her eyes at the pain on her scalp, and she grew nauseated with fear.

"You'd better tell Matt here what you understand, little lady." The leader spoke in tones that were low and ominous.

"I—I—understand," she sobbed. "I—"

"What do you understand?" he asked, leaning closer to her. The presence of the two men pressing against her was suffocating, and she was afraid that any minute she would black out.

"I won't write—I—the story—about—" Her voice broke in another sob. "The story—about—Doug." Tears were rolling freely down her face, but she felt the grip on her hand and hair loosen. Her hand reached up to touch her scalp, then dropped to massage her swollen fingers that had been squeezed so tightly.

"Just make sure you remember it, Miss Ingles, 'cause we're watching you." The tight-lipped one reached out and touched her hair. It was the first time he had touched her, and for some reason it frightened her much more than the brutal grip of the leering one. "It'd be a crying shame to have that pretty little face of yours all messed up, now, wouldn't it?"

He withdrew his hand, and the two men moved away. Their departure was so quick, Kat wasn't even sure which way they had gone. She stared blankly at the car parked next to her van, her left hand still kneading the sore bones of her right. Without her realizing it, Kat's knees collapsed, and her legs buckled beneath her. Sitting on the ground, her body shook with racking sobs, her mind registering nothing but the pain and the shock and the fright brought on by the two men.

Time slipped by unnoticed. The sun was making a rapid descent in the western sky, and an evening chill began to penetrate her bones. Wiping the tears from her face, Kat attempted to stand, but her legs were too weak to support her. A pair of arms reached for her, but she fought wildly against them, berating herself for not getting into the van and locking the door while she could have.

"Katherine, for God's sake, what is it?" She was lifted into strong arms and pulled against a hard, warm chest. Knowing it wasn't the two men who had accosted her earlier, she lifted her red, swollen eyes to look at Doug. Her mouth would form no words. She was so glad to see him, so thankful for his strength and protection, but her voice would make no sound.

When she did speak it was barely above a whisper. "My keys . . ."

"What, honey? What did you say?" He leaned his ear toward her mouth.

"My keys," she began again. "I don't know where they are." As if this fact were the cause of all her problems, her tears broke loose anew, streaming down her face as she held herself dejectedly against Doug.

"It's okay, honey. It's okay." His voice washed over her, soothing and gentle. "I'll find them. Don't worry." Holding her at arm's length, his gaze searched the ground, spotting the keys just under the edge of the van. As Doug stooped to pick them up, Kat's body moved with his to the ground. He dropped the keys into his pocket, then picked her up, cradling her in his arms while he opened the already unlocked van.

He carried her inside and walked to the back of the van, laying her down gently on the couch. Moving back to the door, he pulled it closed and locked it, then reached for a glass in the cabinet and filled it with water.

Bringing it back to her, he lifted her head and brought the glass to her lips, pouring the liquid into her parched mouth.

Within moments Kat's senses returned, and she was wiping the last of the tears from her eyes. She sat up slowly, not yet trusting her stomach to keep its contents down.

"Your hand!" Doug reached down to touch gingerly the bruised fingers of her right hand. "What happened?"

She breathed deeply several times to calm her queasy stomach, and cleared her throat to make sure her voice would make a sound.

"I was—I was just walking back to the van, and these two men . . . they chased me through the parking lot. . . . I was running as fast as I could, but I couldn't get away from them—they just kept coming." Her voice was strident and shaky, her fears still roiling under the surface. "I turned around and they were gone . . . and then I ran to the van, and I tried to unlock it, but at first the key wouldn't work!" Her sore fingers demonstrated in the air how the lock wouldn't turn. "And then this hand . . . it grabbed my fingers and crushed them hard, and they were there. The two men were standing beside me, and one had this ugly twisted mouth, and I was so scared, and I didn't know what to do!"

"It's okay, honey." Doug wrapped her in the circle of his arms, his hand reaching up to stroke the back of her head. "You're safe now."

After a moment her shaking subsided, and she was able

to continue recounting the event. "They said— This one man did all the talking, and he said that if I didn't want to get hurt, I had better"—Kat gazed up at Doug fearfully, wondering what part he was playing in all of this—"I had better drop the story about you."

"What!" His voice exploded into fragments in the tiny confines of the van. His face flashed with such fierce anger and shock that Kat's blood chilled at the dangerous power that seethed beneath the thin facade of the man. "Who were they?" He had grasped her upper arms tightly, but Kat noticed that even with the strength contained in his hands, he did not hurt her. He was not like those other men, finding their power in hurting those who were weaker than they.

"I don't know. They were just so— Wait! One of them was called . . ." Her mind raked through the memory, remembering that leering face so close to hers. "Matt. One of them was named Matt."

At the harsh curse Doug uttered, Kat jumped. She had never seen him so violently angry. He was pacing the van like a caged animal, his hand raking through his hair, his jaw working convulsively. Suddenly he stopped in front of her, squatting before the couch. Laying his hands on her knees, his blue eyes riveted on her face, he asked, "Besides your hand, did they hurt you?"

"No." She touched her scalp automatically. "They pulled my hair kind of hard, but it's okay. It's really okay, Doug." He had reached his hand up to her head, gently massaging her scalp. "Who were they?" she whispered, afraid to know of his involvement in anything sordid.

His jaw hardened. "Don't worry about it. I'll take care of them." He stood and walked toward the door.

"I *am* worried, Doug. What if they come back? They

made some pretty terrible threats. And I'm—I'm worried about you, too. Can't you tell me who they—"

"I said I'll take care of it." He spoke brusquely, then immediately softened his tone. "Katherine, please, just let me take care of this. I don't want you involved any more than you already are. I don't want you to get hurt anymore."

"Why did you come here tonight?" She knew he was going to go, and she wanted more than anything for him to stay. Holding her breath in hopes that his answer would be the one she most wanted to hear, she waited.

Standing by the door, he looked at her for a long moment before answering. "I don't know. I thought maybe I could find someplace to get away from all the suspicious stares and rumblings of gossip for a little while. But"—he laughed bitterly—"I guess here with you isn't really the place for that, is it?"

"Doug, I—"

"Lock your door when I leave." He opened it and started to step down but stopped and turned to face Kat. "Don't worry about those smelly little punks. When I'm through with them, they won't bother anyone . . . ever again."

The anger surging back into his face, Doug stepped down into the night and was gone. Kat jumped from the couch and locked the door behind him. She walked around the van, pulling the curtains closed and making sure that each window was locked tightly.

Lying down on the couch, fully dressed, she stared at the ceiling until sleep overtook her. It was to be a long, restless night before the dawn finally rescued her.

For once Doug was grateful that those two dirty little

bastards had contacted him. He had planned to search every bar and whorehouse in St. Louis until he found them, but he never expected this kind of luck. They came to him. To his hotel room!

After he answered the knock on the door, Doug had to fight down the urge to smash something into their faces as they stared at him calmly from across the threshold.

In contrast to the pure rage that curled inside his stomach, he waved his arm expansively and invited them in. Facing the two men with a blank expression, he leaned his back casually against the door, closing it tight, his fingers twisting the lock quietly until it was secure.

"Ain't you gonna offer us a drink, golden boy?" Rick Manzino said, smirking.

"Yea, Hayden, we wanna drink." The one called Matt forced an obscene laugh from his throat.

Without changing his expression Doug cocked his thumb toward the bathroom. "The toilet's in there. Help yourselves."

Icy silence crackled against the tense air of the room. For a long moment Matt's body coiled as if he were ready to strike. It was Rick who broke the dangerous spell.

"All right, funny boy. Let's talk about why we're here."

"Let's do that." Doug walked away from the door and over to the window, where he stood staring out, as if oblivious to the two men behind him.

"You played real good today, golden boy, real good." Rick was picking at something beneath a fingernail on his left hand. "But then, the game ain't over yet, is it? Two more days. Yes, sir, two more days to go. Let's just hope you keep up the good work, right?"

"I know you're here for more than a pep talk, so I suggest you get on with it." Doug's back was still facing the room but his fist clenched and unclenched repeatedly in front of him. Just a few more minutes. There are two of them, don't forget. The timing has to be just right. Hang on.

"Pep talk." Rick laughed. "That's good, funny boy. That's real good. Ain't that good, Matt?"

"Yeah, that's good, Rick. Yeah." Matt's low, disgusting laugh filled Doug with a vision of Katherine's body being held in his filthy grasp. He began to sweat, his body wanting the release of smashing Matt's face into the floor. But his mind would not yet give the signal. Not yet. Just a little longer.

"What we're here for, pretty boy, is to tell you that we went to visit your girl friend. You remember, the one with the nice . . . well, I guess I don't have to tell you about her, now, do I?"

Doug turned from the window, his eyes and stance so calm, so casual, that Rick should have read the warning signal. But he didn't. He was too busy gloating over what he assumed to be his upper edge.

"We told her to keep her little story about you to herself. I think she got the message. But just in case she didn't, golden boy, you'd better make sure she did."

"What makes you think I have any control over what she does?"

Rick laughed, and there was absolutely no trace of humor in the sound. "Let me put it in plain English for you, golden boy. If you don't control her big mouth, we're gonna do it for you. We've got too good a deal going here, for some sleazy broad to screw it up. And it'd be a cryin' shame for that highfalutin sister of yours to be ruined all because you fell for some cheap broad."

"What makes you so sure that anyone would believe her

story anyway?" Doug said, watching as Matt wandered aimlessly around the room. He was obviously bored with the exchange and ready to move on. That was good. Keep your mind open for something else, you slimy little weasel, and in a minute I'll give you something to think about.

"Oh, we've checked out that Ingles broad. We know what she's up to. You're not the first, pretty boy. No, she's done the same thing to others. You fell for her bait, just like all them others." Rick's laugh sounded this time more like a high-pitched squeak. "Yeah, that broad'll do anything for a story. I realize she's a nice little piece of—"

Now, his mind screamed! Now!

Grasping the small wooden table beside him, Doug hurled it toward the unsuspecting Matt. Caught off guard, the big man was thrown off balance and tumbled over the back of the couch, landing on the floor on the other side. Watching his companion's ungraceful plunge to the floor, Rick missed seeing the fist that flew with sickening speed toward his face. In one bone-splintering crunch Doug slammed his fist against Rick's jaw, forcing the smaller man off his feet. Before Rick could stand, Doug was on him again, repeatedly smashing his knuckles against Rick's flesh.

Recovering from his fall, Matt leaped toward Doug like an angry bull.

After ramming his elbow into Rick's stomach Doug was able to pivot and face his attacker.

Expecting it to take no more than a couple of punches to lay this hotshot golfer low, Matt drew back slightly, relaxing his stance. It was a big mistake.

Slamming his knee into the man's groin, and his painfully swollen hand coming up under Matt's chin, Doug laid the heavier man out flat.

Rick was beginning to stir, so Doug turned back to him. Grabbing him by the collar, he snarled, "You made a big mistake this afternoon, Manzino. And you're not going to live to make another."

Somewhere in the back sectors of his brain Doug heard voices. Loud voices, yelling, commands of some sort. He heard something hitting against the door, harder and harder until, splintering from its hinges, the door crashed into the room.

Someone grabbed his wrist. There were others. They were holding him back. No, just one more time! Let me hit him just one more time!

He was hauled backward, and, slowly, the blazing rage within him subsided to smoldering disgust.

For the first time in recent memory Kat was grateful for such an early awakening. Her dreams had been tortured and violent, switching back and forth from tumultuous sensations of passion to dreams of flight from a variety of tormentors. One moment she was being chased by those hoods who had threatened her in the parking lot. The next minute the man chasing her was Doug, and in the next sequence it was herself, and the threat of being caught was as terrifying as with the other tormentors.

Since she awakened so early, she had plenty of time to shower and eat a leisurely breakfast. She was in no hurry to get to the tournament, and she was certainly in no hurry to leave the van.

By the time she had eaten and cleaned up the dishes, it was time to head for the course to catch the first group teeing off.

She opened the door cautiously and ushered Bogie outside for his morning outing. Closing it quickly behind him, she opened the curtains and scanned the parking lot for any sign of those two characters. She didn't feel any safer in the broad daylight than she had felt at night. After all, they had been bold enough to chase her in the daytime before.

After Bogie returned, greatly relieved from his long confinement in the van, Kat picked up her tote bag and, slinging it over her shoulder, stepped down onto the ground, locking the door behind her.

As she walked across the parking lot toward the press tent, her eyes kept a careful lookout. Never stopping, they moved from side to side, distrustful of what might await her behind every car.

She didn't really want to go to the press tent, as she was still afraid to confront the hostility of the other journalists. But she had to pick up a pairing sheet from the tournament officials, so a trip to the tent was unavoidable.

As she entered, the inevitable hush fell over the group of reporters. Only this time she knew that the usual reaction would not fade as quickly.

"Miss Ingles." She turned to find one of the tournament officials holding a slip of paper for her. "This message came for you yesterday evening, but you had already gone. I didn't know where to contact you."

"Thank you." She took the piece of paper along with her pairing sheet and unfolded it, trying to read the haphazardly scrawled message. It was from her father. He had something important to tell her and asked that she call him as soon as she could.

Not taking the time to puzzle over what the important message could be, Kat walked to the nearest phone and dialed home.

"Hello, Dad?"

"Katy, are you all right?" Her father sounded relieved to hear her voice.

"Yes, I'm fine." She wasn't about to tell him of the episode the night before. Her parents worried enough about her as it was. "I got a message saying you called."

"Yes, yes. I think it must be about that article you're working on, because I got a telephone call from an Elizabeth Hayden. She said she's Doug's sister, and she asked that you contact her. She said it was very important that she talk to you as soon as possible."

Doug's sister? What on earth could she want from Kat? Maybe she had heard somehow about the rumors and wanted to convince Kat not to write the article. Was she to be threatened again? Well, the least she could do was find out what the woman wanted. And she was a part of Doug's family.

"Okay, Dad. Did she give you a number?"

"Yes, just a minute . . . oh, here it is." Her father related the number to her.

"That area code . . . that's a Missouri number, isn't it?"

"Yes, she said she was calling from Sandolia. That's south of where you are."

"Well, thank you, Dad. I'll give her a call."

"Katy"—her father cleared his throat—"I hope that this situation works out. . . ." He cleared his throat once again. "Well, honey, what I'm trying to say is that your mother and I love you and are worried about you."

"I love you both too, Dad. And please don't worry about me. Everything will work out fine."

If only that were true. She wished she could believe it even as she was telling her father it was so. Her life was in such turmoil right then, she didn't know if she would ever get out of the hole she had dug for herself. She hadn't planned for it to happen. She hadn't planned to fall in love with Doug Hayden. And she certainly hadn't counted on being presented with facts that could very well ruin his career. After the way Doug left her van last night, she knew he would never forgive her. And who could blame him? He was lost to her forever. That fact alone made the violent threats made by smelly hoods, the hostility directed toward her by the other journalists, the loss of her credibility as a serious golf reporter, dwindle into paltry insignificance.

After hanging up from the conversation with her father, Kat dialed Doug's sister's number, charging the call to her credit card.

The phone rang twice before a receptionist answered, saying, "Wallace, Hayden, and Winford."

Kat asked for Miss Hayden, and the receptionist promptly transferred the call.

From the tone of her voice Kat could tell that Elizabeth Hayden was highly relieved to have received Kat's call.

"I was afraid you might not call me, Miss Ingles."

"Please call me Kat. I don't think I understand why you want to talk to me. You're Doug's sister, is that right?"

"Yes, and it's that story—of Doug's *alleged* cheating on the Tour—that I simply must talk to you about."

"I know what you must think of me, Miss Hayden, but I've had my share of threats and criticism over this story, so—"

"Miss . . . Kat, I don't want to threaten you or criticize you for what you're doing. I'm sure you think you're doing the right thing. But I have some information for you that might change your opinion of Doug and . . . and I hope clear his name."

"Okay, I'm willing to listen to anything you have to say.

I hope you'll believe me when I tell you that I'd do anything to clear Doug's name."

"I know you would, Kat. Uh, Doug has . . . talked to me about you. But there is a snag to all of this. I can't explain the information over the phone. I have to see you in person. If you could come here, I'd pay for your gas. It's only a two-hour drive from St. Louis, and if I could get away without being noticed, I would come there instead of asking you to drive here. Is—is it possible for you to do that?"

"Well . . . I suppose I could." Kat wondered at the information this woman would have that might straighten out Doug's rapidly declining reputation. And what did she mean, if she could get away without being noticed? Well, the only way to find out was to drive down there and talk to her.

"I'll leave right away, Miss Hayden."

CHAPTER TEN

"Doug has always been that way, making my problems his problems."

Elizabeth Hayden and Kat Ingles were sitting together in a quiet booth in a nondescript and near-empty café on Main Street.

Sandolia was a small town, with a population of ten thousand. The courthouse perched like a roosting chicken on a grassy mound at the end of the street, and the rest of the buildings on the street all joined together in two rows of unassuming uniformity. Kat had met Elizabeth at her law office in the beige stone building adjacent to the courthouse.

From the moment they met they had been able to relate as if they had known each other for a long time. Easygoing like her brother, but with a slightly more serious bent, Elizabeth suggested they talk at the café over a cup of coffee. "As you can see," she said when they first sat down, "very little I say or do is kept confidential." She pointed to a campaign poster with her photograph and the slogan TIME FOR A CHANGE. VOTE ELIZABETH HAYDEN FOR MAYOR in the window. "That's why I couldn't go to St. Louis. I can't go anywhere without everyone wondering what I'm up to," she whispered conspiratorially.

Tall and attractive like her brother, Elizabeth was also

articulate and well-educated, all of which she attributed to Doug.

"You see, our parents died when we were in grade school." Kat sipped her coffee, watching Elizabeth's face as she reflected on the past. "My mother's brother took us into his family. I don't want to sound ungrateful toward my uncle in any way, because he certainly didn't have to do it. We could have been placed in an orphanage, or Doug and I could have been split apart. So, I'm very grateful that he allowed us to become a part of his family." Elizabeth smiled before continuing.

"But, there *were* problems. He was quite wealthy and was able to give both of us all the material things we could possibly want. We had good educations, and Doug was given the opportunity to learn golf, which, as I'm sure you know, is not an inexpensive sport."

"Oh, yes, that I *do* know," Kat concurred, remembering the expense of new golf clubs, lessons, green fees, and clothes.

"That's right. Doug mentioned that you were a golf pro at one time."

"No." Kat's mouth twisted. "Just an amateur."

"That was how you met, wasn't it?"

Clearing her throat, Kat flushed, wondering exactly how much Doug had told his sister about them. "Uh, yes," she mumbled.

"Well . . ." Elizabeth sighed. "I guess I'm getting off the track a bit. Anyway, our uncle provided for us quite well in some respects, but not so well in others. He was in his late forties when we went to live with him and his family, and his children were already in college. So he didn't have much time for our emotional development. Doug, being four years older than myself, assumed the role of father to me. Do you have any older brothers or sisters, Kat?"

"No, I'm an only child." She had always wanted a brother or sister, but despite her nagging as a young child, her parents had continued to insist—without her having the slightest hint of what they were talking about—that for them another child was an impossibility.

"Doug was no angel when he was young." Elizabeth smiled to herself. "He got into his share of trouble. But he seemed to know when to quit and just how far to go. Whereas with me it was just the opposite. I'd barge into trouble without a thought of the consequence. And it was always Doug who saved me from punishment, taking the blame himself or relating my actions to our uncle in such a humorous way that I nearly always escaped the penalty."

"Your own guardian angel." Kat laughed, trying to imagine what Doug must have been like as a child.

"Yes and no." Elizabeth chuckled. "You see, I may have escaped my uncle's form of punishment, but I didn't escape Doug's. Once he got me alone, he really let me have it. The reprimand I received from him made it very clear that I'd better not commit that particular infraction again."

Remembering Doug's anger of the night before, Kat could certainly believe that underneath the easygoing facade was a man who demanded control and discipline. "But you said earlier that the problems he's having now are your fault. I don't see—"

"I know you must think I'm beating around the bush, Kat, but I thought that a little background might help you understand better the relationship between my brother and myself."

"No, don't hurry! I want to learn . . . I want to know everything there is to know about Doug." Kat's cheeks flushed a bright red. She hadn't intended to reveal her personal involvement with Doug in front of his sister. And yet there was something about Elizabeth Hayden that made it impossible to hold back. "I really know so little about him," Kat added softly.

"That is the truth!" Elizabeth spoke a bit harshly. Immediately her expression softened contritely. "I'm sorry if that sounded rude, Kat. It's just that no one knows the real Doug. The Doug Hayden the world sees is a product of media hype, not the real man." She paused, looking out the window for a long moment.

"Do you know that I love him, Elizabeth?" Kat was again startled to find herself divulging this information, but she wanted Elizabeth to know that she wasn't unfeeling, that she wasn't just out to get a story.

"I know that." When Elizabeth turned back to Kat her smile was reflected in her eyes as well as her mouth. "And I also know how Doug feels about you."

Kat's eyes focused sharply on the other woman, her mind trying to fathom what information had passed between brother and sister.

"I've never seen him so affected by a woman." Elizabeth shook her head in wonder. "I mean, Doug has had his share of romances . . . good and bad. But this time it's different. You know, Kat, when he told me how you two first met and the—uh—circumstances, I started understanding some things I hadn't before.

"Three years ago, before his divorce, I knew he had met someone special, but I didn't know who, of course. I remember, when he'd come to visit, how he'd pace the floor at night. He was really hurting, but he wouldn't let me help. When I asked him if it was another woman he said yes, but that's all he'd say about it. He was like a caged animal, repeating constantly that he had to make Melissa give him a divorce. It was a very painful time for him. Of course, now I know that that other woman was you, Kat."

Too stunned to speak for several minutes, Kat stared out the window. If only she had known how he felt before all of this. If only he had told her! "I'm afraid all of that is past tense now." Kat knew what Doug thought of her now. The night before, he had made that perfectly clear. He could not find the peace he wanted with her. She had betrayed him for the things she thought she wanted in life, and it was too late to reverse the harm she had done.

"Well, perhaps." Elizabeth paused for a long moment. "I don't know. Maybe it is too late for you two to work out whatever problems there are between you, but I'm hoping that it's not too late to rectify the damage that's been done to Doug's career. I have to admit, when I first learned of the rumor and of your part in it, I didn't think I liked the woman named Kat Ingles very much."

The two women looked at each other for a drawn-out second, weighing each other's motives and personalities.

"I think we're very much alike, Kat," Elizabeth concluded. "We're both striving to make it in fields that are dominated by men. I'm sure that in the path I've forged, I've broken a few branches on the way. So I can't blame you entirely for what's happened. But then"—she laughed, taking a sip of her now-cold coffee—"I haven't even told you what's happening, have I?"

Before she began Elizabeth signaled the waitress to refill their cups with fresh coffee. After the young girl poured the steaming liquid into their cups and returned to her post behind the counter, Elizabeth resumed her story in a voice only one breath above a whisper.

"When I was in high school, Doug was already in college, of course. Since I no longer had my guardian angel, as you called him, around to protect me, I began falling into trouble continuously. I started hanging around a wild group of kids and dating a boy who was what we called a thug back in those days.

"His name was Rick Manzino, and I have to admit I found his wild ways pretty exciting after being protected by mother hen Doug for so long. Succumbing to Rick's pressure, I got involved in some illegal activities. I was arrested one night." She stopped, sighing deeply, her face pulled together in painful reflection. She looked back at Kat. "The charge was petit larceny, and because I was a minor with no previous offenses, I was let off the hook pretty easily. With the judge, that is. When Doug found out"—her eyes rolled upward—"well, I don't have to tell you what hit the fan immediately."

"That bad, huh?" Kat smiled sadly, knowing how painful it must be for this woman to open her past to a stranger this way.

"Worse!" she exclaimed. "But after the fire died down, he helped me straighten myself out and somehow managed to have the offense taken off my record. Don't ask me how he did it." She raised her hands in surrender. "I'm not sure I really want to know. But anyway, he did it.

"So, after high school, I went to college and got my law degree, and now I'm running for mayor of this town I call home. Sounds like a happy ending, doesn't it?" Her eyes closed briefly with a painful thought.

Kat knew it was best to say nothing, to let Elizabeth tell

her story in her own way, without questions or input from someone else.

"A few months ago Rick Manzino contacted Doug and threatened to destroy my campaign unless Doug did what he wanted. He remembered me and found out I was running for mayor here, and I guess he thought it would be an easy way to make some money.

"According to Doug, he's not a big-time crook in the underworld. He's just some punk who wants to try and drag the rest of the world down to his gutter level. Anyway, he apparently runs a bookie joint in Kansas City, and, by laying odds or something, he's trying to attract some of the big gamblers to his business. He and another two-bit hood told Doug he had better start winning tournaments any way he could, or they would reveal my past criminal record to the public."

"But you said it was never put on your record," Kat interjected.

"That's true. But just the allegation is enough to destroy any chances I have of becoming mayor of this town. Keep in mind, Kat, this isn't Chicago or Detroit, where voters will often overlook certain 'discrepancies' in your record as long as you can make their subways and buses run. This is 'Small Town USA,' the heart of the Midwest. The voters in this town don't want even a trace of scandal in their mayoral race. They want to elect someone who is an upstanding citizen, attends church every Sunday, lives in a house no better than their own, and drives a two-year-old sedan."

"Hmm, I see what you mean. But surely there was something Doug could do, besides cheat, to win."

"Hold on, Kat. You're getting ahead of me. I never said

he did cheat. I only said they told him he'd better win, even if he had to cheat."

"But he's won four of the last five tournaments," Kat pointed out.

"All I can say to that is that something or someone is watching over Doug Hayden. Call it Lady Luck, if you will. But so far he's been able to win on his own merits."

"But what happens if he falls behind and knows there's no chance of winning without cheating?" Kat asked, not sure she wanted to hear the answer.

"He would cheat." Elizabeth Hayden tilted her chin high, but her eyes misted over with tears. "That's the kind of brother, the kind of man, he is, Kat. He would do anything to protect me, including destroying his own career."

Kat stared at the woman, numbed to the bone. To have someone love you that much. To give up everything he had worked for, to destroy his reputation, all for a sister whom he loved and wanted to protect.

"That's why I called you, Kat." Elizabeth was wiping at the tears on her cheeks. "I—I can't let that happen. I want this post as mayor. I want it so bad I can taste it. But I don't want it at the expense of my brother's career. He has worked . . . so hard to get where he is. Golf is everything to him, Kat." Elizabeth stopped to clear the lump from her throat. "So I've decided that I'm going to the local newspaper and tell them the story."

"Elizabeth!" Kat was appalled that circumstances between a brother and sister who loved each other so deeply could take away all they had worked and dreamed for.

"It's the only way, Kat. Doug cannot keep winning forever, and I will not have him throw away everything he has worked so hard for. I'll tell my story and just hope—

and pray—that the people of this town will find it in their hearts to understand, or at least forgive. If not . . . well, I've still got my law practice. And, more important, I won't be living a lie."

Kat had been staring angrily at her typewriter for over an hour. The frustration was there, the anger was there, but she hadn't been able to get it out yet. It was as if a huge bubble was building inside her and that at any minute it was going to burst with a devastating explosion.

She had so often used writing as an outlet for her emotions. Getting it outside her body always seemed to help somehow. The problem was still there, but once it was outside of herself, she could deal with it better.

That's what she wanted then. She wanted to get it out. It was hurting too much. She had to get something down on paper. There was so much she wanted to say, so much that needed to be aired. Never had she been so angry about a situation. Never had she encountered firsthand this kind of sacrifice between two people: Elizabeth Hayden, who was about to destroy any chance she might have of becoming mayor, to save her brother's reputation; and Doug Hayden, willing to compromise his integrity and ruin his career, all to protect the sister he loved.

Suddenly the pressure within her began to boil. The guilt, the pain, the regret, she had been carrying around for a month began to spill forth onto the clean white paper in the typewriter. Time moved by quietly without her knowledge of its passing. She was so absorbed in the details of the story that she did not notice that the lunch hour had long since passed and that it was approaching dusk.

When she finished typing she sat at the table, staring

vacantly at the paper for a long time. It was all down on paper, everything, and she felt as if nothing was left inside of her. She had nothing more to give, and she had nothing to put back inside of herself. It was a strange feeling, this emptiness.

If only she could talk to Doug, to explain to him . . . no, it would do no good. He had made it perfectly clear the night before that he could find no peace with her. She had done enough damage. She mustn't, she wouldn't, bother him anymore.

With a heavy depression weighing on her mind, which contrasted with the emptiness she felt inside her body, she started the van and headed back toward St. Louis. The dark road ahead of her stretched as bleak and empty as her future. While only a month ago she had been amazed at the crystal clarity of things, now she saw that the threads of her life had been cruelly raveled into a murky web of obscurity.

All the way back she had been thinking about what she could do to help Doug and Elizabeth. Something had to be done! Those two hoods had to be stopped.

She was just reaching the southern outskirts of St. Louis when the full impact of Doug's words the night before hit her. "When I'm through with them, they won't bother anyone . . . ever again. When I'm through with them . . . ." What was he planning? What was he going to do?

Her foot automatically increased its pressure on the accelerator pedal. She had to reach him! She had to stop him before he did something . . . before he got hurt. Surely he wasn't going to confront those two men himself! Her foot pressed harder, the van straining to meet the demands of its driver.

As she took the exit off the freeway her palms were

perspiring with her effort to get to Doug as quickly as possible. The more she thought about it, the more she realized Doug would probably try to tackle those two guys himself. But, damn! Why hadn't she thought of it before? Last night she had been so frightened and aware of her own danger that she had thought of nothing else. And today her mind had been centered on those facts revealed by Elizabeth Hayden. Please, Doug, don't do anything foolish! She had to hurry.

She knew that no one would be at the country club at this late hour, so she headed directly for the hotel where most of the players were staying. Squeezing into the parking lot, she was out of the van almost before it stopped running.

She dashed into the lobby and up to the reception desk, her voice breathlessly weak. "What room is Doug Hayden in, please?" As if the desk clerk didn't understand her, she repeated the question. "Doug Hayden's room . . . what room number . . . please!"

"I'm sorry, madam, but we can't give out that information. If you would give me your name, I will try to get a message to his room. What did you say the name was?"

"Hayden. Doug Hayden."

The clerk checked through the roster of guests' names.

"Hayden, no . . . He checked out this morning. I'm sorry."

"Checked out! Why would he do that? The tournament isn't over until tomorrow." Turning from the desk, Kat scanned the lobby frantically, hoping to catch a glimpse of one of the other players. The bar. She could try there.

Without another glance at the clerk, Kat hurried through the lobby to the bar at the other end. As she stepped over the threshold, the loud sounds of disco and rock music vibrated around her, and she had to stand still inside the doorway for several minutes before her eyes could adjust to the darkness.

Several male heads at the bar turned to stare at the distraught-looking woman who had just entered all alone. Each of them watched her with his own private thoughts as to what his chances might be.

Before any of them had the opportunity to try their luck, Kat moved over to a table by the dance floor, where she spotted Mike Talbot and Skip Steele, two of the players on the Tour.

"Mike, Skip?" Kat stood awkwardly before them, her hands wringing nervously in front of her. They stared at her as if they had never seen her before. "I'm Kat Ingles. I was wondering—"

"We know who you are." Skip spoke, and his voice was filled with disdain.

So, this was the way it was to be. Well, she couldn't really blame them. After all, in their minds, she had eaten away at the fabric of their noble male bastion. They didn't know that she had been trapped into this situation, that she had never wanted to pursue it in the first place. But she also knew that if no golfer would talk with her, her career as a golf journalist was over. There wasn't much point in wasting her breath trying to explain her true feelings to these guys. Right then, she just wanted to find Doug.

"Where is Doug?"

"You mean you don't know?" Mike sneered.

"No, that's why I'm asking." She was rapidly losing her patience with these two.

"He's gone."

"What do you mean gone?"

"I mean he's off the Tour. He was arrested last night for smearing his hotel room with two guys."

"Arrested!" Oh, God, why hadn't she thought to stop him sooner? "He's in jail?"

"No, he was released, but he's off the Tour, pending an investigation. I guess you were right all along, Miss Ingles. You should be quite proud of yourself." Mike's derisive tone hardened to steel. "Those two guys Hayden put in the hospital claimed he tried to shut them up. Said they had some proof against him that the tournament officials would be highly interested in."

"It's a lie!" she cried, causing heads at several tables to turn toward her. "They were blackmailing him. It's a lie! He never cheated!"

"Come on, Kat. Just because you didn't get your exclusive story, don't cry around about it. I'm sure you'll find some more smut somewhere to dig up."

She didn't hear what else they had to say. She didn't want to hear. All she had tried to do was make an independent life for herself. To have a career and a man. Wanting the best of both worlds, she had tried to play the game—and she had lost.

She turned away from the men and walked out the door of the bar. But the discordant sounds of their derisive laughter struck her ears with painful acuity.

There was nothing left for her to do but return home once again to the security of her family. There she could lose herself in the fantasy of the coming holidays, surrounded by the fragile cocoon of memories that she could find only in her own home.

CHAPTER ELEVEN

The holiday season was in what is officially known as "full swing." It was Thanksgiving, and Kat had spent the morning helping her mother prepare the turkey, dressing, and pies and all afternoon trying to digest them. Invited for dinner were a half-dozen relatives from the Kansas City area. The afternoon was whiled away by all doing nothing more consequential than sitting in overstuffed chairs, their bodies in overstuffed conditions.

Then, at seven thirty in the evening, she was huddled next to the outside brick wall of Hall's chic department store, hoping to find a buffer against the cold November wind. Hundreds of other people had gathered for the same reason she had this night—to bask in the glow of the annual Christmas light ceremony at The Plaza.

Hugging her coat tighter to her body, she stared out through the cold night air. She was waiting. Waiting for the lights of the shopping plaza to explode with sparkling brilliance against the dark sky. Waiting for a sense of peace that had not yet come, even though she had been home for two months. Waiting.

It had been a month earlier when Kat began to face the fact that happiness was beyond her reach. It left her devoid of all feeling. She was hollow inside, knowing that because of her pride and blind ambition, she had lost the two things in life she wanted the most. She had lost Doug, and she had lost her career as a golf journalist.

She was fully aware that no golf editor would use her again after her mutinous stance with one of them, Jack Lichtenstein.

"I won't apologize for this," she had written in the note to the editor. "If a magazine is not responsible enough to print the truth, it's not worthy of a readership that wants the facts."

Had she really written that to Jack? She still cringed every time she thought of what she had done. Just before she sent the note to the editor, the investigation into Doug's alleged cheating had begun, and Kat could not seem to lift the weight of guilt and sorrow from her shoulders.

She knew that Doug had come back to Kansas City, too, but she didn't know where he was living. After talking to his sister, Kat knew that Doug had not used her to buy her silence. He had cared, and Kat had been so full of pride, so fearful of humiliation, that she had chosen to believe the worst in him rather than the best. She'd had her chance and then it was gone.

It had been two o'clock in the morning, on the day, two and a half weeks earlier, when it had finally dawned on her that she couldn't just continue pacing the floors, crying, and damning herself. She had to do something to help Doug. She had rummaged through the papers on her desk until she came across what she had written that day after talking to Elizabeth Hayden.

It was all there. The whole scenario. The circumstances between Doug Hayden and his sister were laid out clearly. What she had written was much too emotional to be considered a good piece of journalistic writing, but it was what needed to be said. Kat's own guilt and pain were evident under the surface of the words, but to remove that would be to destroy what the essay was trying to say. As she read through it she tried to remember writing all of it but couldn't. Where had the deep emotion come from? Had it really come from inside her?

She had dealt with how external pressures on golfers affect their game, their attitudes, and their careers. She had touched on the manner in which some golfers stand up to the pressures, sometimes putting their careers in jeopardy. But the underlying point of it—a written confession was the only way she could describe it—was that within each golfer was a person whose basic morality was determined by their commitment not to golf, but to the people in their personal lives. And that if that moral integrity existed in their personal lives, it would carry over to their other pursuits.

She had also vented clearly her anger and frustration over the shallow and fickle attitudes of the fans. Everyone was so ready to believe the worst of Doug Hayden, so unwilling to wait until the actual verdict was in. No, they wouldn't wait. They were already hanging the noose across the old oak tree. Packing up the picnics and the babies, they were all set for the carnival lynching.

When she had stuffed the papers—without a single change or rewrite—into an envelope with the note to the editor, and had wet the glue on the flap, she had known that she was sealing her fate. Her career as a golf journalist was over.

But it hadn't mattered anymore. She had made the biggest mistake she could ever make. She had pushed aside her own basic morality and beliefs, set love aside, all for the sake of furthering her career. And after she had sold her soul for that goal, she no longer wanted it. She couldn't care less if she ever wrote about another golfer or tournament as long as she lived.

And she didn't care what Jack Lichenstein, or any other editor for that matter, thought about her. She had compromised her principles too long, and she would do it no longer. She nearly ruined a man's life—maybe *did* ruin it—and she tried her best to rectify the damage she had done.

Two weeks later, when the editor called her from New York, Kat couldn't have been more surprised.

"We love it, Kat. . . . No, not a word . . . we're not changing a word of it. . . . It's the best we've seen in quite awhile. We want you as a permanent member of our staff. . . . Yes, salaried assignments and transportation expenses. Don't say no yet . . . just think about it for a little while . . . but not too long now. . . . We don't want any of our competitors stealing you away from us."

Even now—standing at The Plaza in the cold night air, waiting, hoping for the Christmas display to fill her with a sense of purpose, a sense of belonging—Kat could not believe what had happened with her article.

Jack had meant what he had said about not changing a word. They had even included her letter to the editor, printing it at the beginning of the article. She had been inundated with calls from other golf reporters, all of whom were full of praise and encouragement. Her status, it seemed, had changed overnight. She was no longer the pariah of the golf-writing business. She was in demand. She was accepted. She had achieved the one thing she had always wanted. But, ironically, the taste of success was now like acid on her tongue.

Doug had since sailed victoriously through the investigation before the TPA officials. When it was over, his reputation was as solid as it had been before the incident began, and he was now back on the Tour, finishing third in the previous week's tournament at Pebble Beach. Whether her article had anything to do with his success with the officials or whether it was strictly Elizabeth Hayden's disclosure, Kat didn't know. She knew, through her parents, that he had tried to call her several times. When he was going to be on the road, he had even left a number where he could be reached. But she never contacted him. It was better that way. She'd had more than her share of opportunities to love him and to show him that she believed in him. She was happy for him that everything had worked out well in the end, and now he could resume his career and his life the way he wanted without any more interference from her.

She had received a very contrite letter from Tim also, and he was hoping that he would see her at the next tournament. He wouldn't. That part of her life was behind her; she had no desire to go back and pick it up again.

The rumblings of the crowd brought Kat out of her reverie. It was almost time. At precisely eight o'clock the lights blazed on, bathing The Plaza in the dazzling glow of the Christmas season.

As the mob of people around her expressed their admiration for the display of lights, Kat felt as isolated from them as she had before. She had been hoping for the spirit of Christmas to take hold of her the way it used to, but in that she was disappointed. All spirit was gone from her.

But from somewhere deep inside the hollow space that was her heart came the driving need to see Doug one more time. It had nothing to do with hope but everything to do with need. If she had that one chance to see him, she wouldn't bother him, she promised herself that. All she wanted was to see him. Just to look at him once again!

She turned and walked away from the bright lights of Christmas cheer, heading up the desolate, darkened street that led to her parked van.

The reporters were all there for the Oak Ridge Invitational's final press conference, inundating the winners with their usual stale questions. Doug used to enjoy these press conferences. But then, he used to enjoy golf, too. He had come in second, and he felt good about that. It had been a tough course and had taken its toll on all the players, so he felt lucky to have done as well as he had. But something was missing.

He looked out at the sea of faces, hoping to catch sight of that one fair face framed by red hair, the one he had been waiting through so many of these dreary press conferences to see. She was the element that brought the interviews alive. Without her the "thrill of victory" was nothing more than a sports announcer's bombastic myth.

He had made so many mistakes with Kat. He realized that now. Because of him, she had given up her career. And yet, ironically, because of her article, she had probably saved his.

He remembered how, at other press conferences, her eyes would flash wickedly as she tried to prick away at his media image. He had loved those confrontations, and, because his pride had been hurt when he thought she didn't believe in him, those playful conflicts would be no more.

Though he still looked for her each time, he knew he would not see her. He had learned not to hope too much.

The reporter's question to him shifted Doug's mind

back to harsh reality. "On number eighteen, Doug, were you expecting to make that in one putt, or did you think it would take two?"

Forcing his face into a smile, Doug answered. "One thing I've learned only recently, gentlemen, is never to expect anything."

Kat stood among the throng of spectators gathered at the Kansas City store of one of the world's largest sporting-goods chains and watched the golfing demonstration in painful silence, afraid even to breathe lest she give herself away. Her heart was pounding erratically, and the electrical storm of desire that blazed through her body at the sight of him left her weak and dazed. She had promised herself she wouldn't bother Doug. She wanted just to see him. It was a need that had been too strong to deny. She would watch the demonstration and then leave.

Was she hoping to find some fault in his character that would make it easier to turn away? If so, she was flatly disappointed.

He was more handsome than ever. His tan defied winter's paling chill, and his sky-blue eyes sparkled as if he were standing in the bright sunlight rather than under the false lights of the store. She watched with envy as he combed his fingers carelessly through his sandy hair, wishing that she could let her own hand glide through the thick, sun-kissed strands.

As he talked with casual ease to reporters and fans and demonstrated the different swinging techniques, Kat's eyes were drawn magnetically to his strong, agile body as it pivoted and moved with the club's forward and backward motion. God, to feel that body against her again! To be able to touch him and have him touch her one more time!

Her palms had begun to sweat, and she wiped them against her corduroy jeans to remove the moisture. What if she couldn't control herself? What if she burst through the crowd and ran up to him, throwing her arms around him foolishly and begging him to forgive her, to love her? She shouldn't have come here! She should have stayed away from him so that she could forget. But she could never, would never, forget. He was to be a part of her forever, and nothing she could do would ever erase his searing brand from her being.

A flash of red hair in the periphery of his vision caught Doug's attention. Glancing up, he saw her, and it was as though the bubble of need that had been growing in him for so long finally burst. It was too good to be true! He had been trying to figure out how he could make her answer his calls. But to see her again—he hadn't expected that kind of fortune. Had she come to talk? Had she decided finally to stop evading him, to stop ignoring his attempts to reach her?

At the sudden crystal silence in the room, Kat glanced up from the floor. Doug was staring at her! He saw her! She should run, but her legs wouldn't move. She was rooted to this spot. Her gaze locked with his, and his blue eyes impaled her with shining intensity, and his mouth parted ever so slightly as if he might say something to her. What was it in his eyes? What was burning in those two blue flames? It was a different expression from the one she had seen before in them. What was it?

She stopped trying to register in her mind what his eyes were saying. What was the point? She knew that she had blown her chance with him. She didn't need for him to tell her that. Her pain was great enough without subjecting herself to his piercing scrutiny. She shouldn't have come. It was a big mistake!

The reporter from the television station that was holding the press conference cleared his throat nervously as he glanced back and forth from Doug to the young woman in the crowd. He fidgeted with his equipment, blowing nervously into his microphone as if testing it for its performance. Again clearing his throat, his voice shook. "Mr. Hayden . . . uh, could you—could you tell us what—what is the most important aspect of making a good shot?" The last part of the question came out in a breathless flow, as if the young reporter were relieved to have gotten it all out.

Doug tried to hide his anxiety as he watched Kat turn and begin weaving through the crowd, pushing her way to the store's exit. His eyes darted back and forth from the reporter to the crowd, keeping tabs on where she was at each second. "The most important thing . . ." He spoke by rote, having answered the question at least a thousand times before. But his eyes were trained on Kat as she pulled open the door and stepped into that framed rectangle of winter. ". . . is to keep your eye on the ball." Damn! He had let her go too many times before. He wouldn't, he couldn't, do it again.

"To hell with the ball!" At that moment he dropped his golf club to the floor and began moving through the startled crowd, the reporter left behind holding his microphone in stunned disbelief.

Moving as quickly as possible through the jostling crowd, Doug reached the doorway, flinging it open and dashing out into the gray, wintry chill. Not a trace of sunlight filtered through the sky's ashen pallor.

Doug glanced to the left, then to the right. Which way

had she gone? Hundreds of people, it seemed, were in his line of vision, returning Christmas gifts and taking advantage of after-holiday sales.

He wended his way through the crowd at The Plaza, looking frantically in every direction. And then he saw her. She had lifted the hood of her fur-lined parka up over her head, but he had caught the flash of red hair just before it was covered. He ran to the left, apologizing automatically as he pushed his way through the shoppers.

Kat was heading briskly up the street to the area where she had managed to find a space in which to squeeze the van. What a terrible mistake she had made! Why had she gone there? She thought that if she could see him once more, she might be able to face the hopelessness of their relationship. But she couldn't. Though his life had obviously gone on quite nicely without her, she had been tortured each and every day by the memories of him.

Would she ever be able to face life without him? She would have to. She had to start making her way in society again. She had to face the fact that her life was to be lived without Doug Hayden playing an active part in it. He would remain in her memory, in her dreams, and in her desires. But he would not ever be an active component of her everyday life. You have to face up to that fact, Kat. Damn it, once and for all accept it!

"Katherine!" Her name splintered through the ice-laden air. "Katherine!" She turned, knowing that voice but afraid to believe it was really his. Hugging her coat against her in an involuntary gesture of self-protection, she waited, watching warily as Doug tried to catch his breath and restore the warm air to his lungs. He started to touch her, almost reached out to stroke her arm, but his hand stopped in midair when she stepped back.

She couldn't let him touch her. It had been bad enough seeing him again, but if she felt his hand on her, she might never get over it.

"Katherine, we've got to talk." Doug's blue eyes had turned to slate against the gray sky, and she could now see the shadows under them and the weary glaze covering the once-brilliant irises.

She remembered the last time he had said that to her, the day they had almost made love on the golf course. Is that what he was actually saying when he said we have to talk? That he wanted to have sex with her? Is that what she should be reading in the depths of those eyes?

"You don't have to do that, Doug. I think enough has been said—"

"Nothing has been said." He spoke too harshly, then grimaced and softened his tone. "None of the right things have been said."

"All right," she agreed with hesitation. "We can talk . . . if you want."

"If I want?" His eyes narrowed on her. Had he read her wrong? Had he believed mistakenly that she wanted the same thing he did? No! She was still hurt, that's all. And it was blocking her up, making her afraid to face the truth about their relationship. "What do you want, Katherine?"

God! Don't ask a question like that, Doug. You can't even begin to imagine what I want. She wasn't about to tell him the truth and take the chance of having him laugh at her, or, even worse, make a politely conscious effort to let her down easily. No, she could never tell him the way she really felt. She had missed her chance for that. But she had to answer him with something.

"I guess I want us to be just friends, Doug." She glanced

at him and then quickly looked away before she could tell what he was thinking.

"I think it's too late for that." He looked off toward some of the elegant homes situated on hills that surrounded The Plaza, his eyes hidden from Kat's view. But she noticed the grim tightness that seized the skin around his mouth. She felt heavy, weighted with a burden that she didn't want to face. What he said left little room for hope. It was too late for them to be even friends. He couldn't have been clearer than that.

She looked at him, and he was smiling at her. Gently. Her worst fears were coming true. He was going to be polite and gentle as he crushed her meaningless existence into oblivion. How was she going to get through this scene?

She would have to face it like an adult, that's all. She would try to carry it off with dignity and class.

"Come on, let's get out of the cold. My car is over here." She hesitated for a moment and then let him take her arm and lead her over to a brand-new Lincoln Continental.

"What do you think?" he asked, holding the door open for her.

"It's—it's large."

"Yeah, I know. I hate it, too." He tried to laugh but couldn't quite manage it, then walked to the other side of the car and climbed in behind the wheel. "I let the salesman talk me into it. He thought it went with my image."

She glanced at him with a look of surprise.

"What?" he asked, noticing her wide-eyed expression.

"Oh, nothing." She quickly lowered her lashes, taking in every trivial detail and appointment of the car's interior. "I'm just surprised that anyone could talk you into anything, that's all."

"Hmm. Well, at the time, I had a lot on my mind, I guess. I wasn't feeling too strong in the self-confidence department."

She looked out the window to keep from looking at him. He had pulled onto the street and was driving southwest. She was taken aback by the admission that he had lacked self-confidence. She had never thought she would hear Doug Hayden say something like that. It took a pretty big man to admit his own weaknesses.

"What about your Porsche?" She inserted the inane question to keep her mind from thinking too much about the deeper aspects of Doug's personality.

"Oh, I've still got it, and as soon as I can get this white elephant off my hands, I'll take the dustcover off the Porsche and start driving it again."

He merged the car onto the freeway, still heading southwest. "I thought we could go to my place. I have a town house in Shawnee Mission." His voice was a little shaky. He too was wondering what the outcome of this chance encounter was going to be.

"You don't have to do that, Doug." Kat had noticed the slight hesitation in his voice, and she knew he thought it was what he should do, not what he wanted to do.

"Yes, I do, Katherine." He looked at her briefly, intensely, before turning his attention back to the heavy traffic flow on the freeway.

The rest of the drive was made in awkward silence, each with his or her own thoughts as to what the other was thinking. The low hum of the motor moaned through the car's interior like a funeral dirge.

Kat tried to keep her mind on the scenery outside the car rather than dwelling on the much more magnificent sight inside that seemed to upset her pulse rate so.

It had been a hard winter throughout the nation, and Kansas City had felt the cruel brunt of it. In a way it had been a blessing to Kat. She needed to have something on which to blame her foul mood, and the rotten weather had proven to be the perfect outlet.

And too, she wanted to atone for her part in Doug's troubled career. The punishment of seeing nothing but gray, icy days had simply taken over where her self-flagellation left off.

Kat's mind was so far away, she hadn't realized that they had exited the freeway and were now turning into a private, tree-lined lane of very exclusive town houses. Even with their branches bare, the elm trees draped across the road provided a muffling darkness that seemed to insulate Doug and Kat from the howling winter.

Doug eased the Lincoln into the aggregate driveway and clicked off the motor. He turned toward Kat and started to speak. She waited, breathlessly, but was disappointed when he changed his mind. He climbed out of the car and walked around to help her out. He led her to the door and ushered her in.

The house was elegant, but solidly masculine. There were no frills, no unnecessary art objects, no feminine touches. It was totally male, and almost defiant in its unbending austerity. The furniture was a blend of browns and beiges, complemented by lots of wood and greenery. But one of the first things she noticed was the lack of any golf memorabilia or awards. "This is beautiful, Doug. But where are all your trophies?"

"Oh, they're in a closet somewhere," he mumbled, and shrugged his shoulders.

"Why don't you have them out on display?" She

couldn't understand why he wouldn't want to show them off.

"Look, Katherine, I know you think that the only thing I care about is golf, but it's not!" He hadn't meant for it to sound that way, that harsh. He reached out his hand to apologize, but she had turned away toward the bar. God, she must really detest him.

She grasped the edge of the bar tightly, her emotions stinging from his retort. She hadn't meant to imply that golf was all he cared about. God, he must really hate her.

"Doug." "Katherine." They both turned and spoke at once. They laughed awkwardly. "You go ahead," Doug insisted.

"No, it wasn't important. You go ahead." It *had* been important. She wanted to tell him how sorry she was for the trouble she had caused him over the cheating scandal. She wanted to tell him how sorry she was about Elizabeth. Why in the hell did she say it wasn't important?

"I just wanted to say that I've missed you, Katherine. I've really . . . missed you." His voice was low and soft, no uncertainty evident in his statement.

She stared at him for a long moment, not knowing what to say or think. What did he mean by that? Did he mean that he had simply missed her body, the sexual relationship they had? Or had he missed *her*?

Doug closed the space between them, walking over to the bar, where he placed his hands against its edge, on either side of her. His eyes were no longer dull. They had taken on the brilliance of fire, the desire in them no longer hidden.

She was right. He *had* missed only their sexual relationship, nothing else. She turned her head to the side, trying to avoid the heated stare.

"Katherine, don't close me out. Please." His voice had taken on an urgency that wasn't there before. His hands lifted to her shoulders, removing her coat from her body. She seemed to have no resoluteness of her own, no strength to resist his will. She let him remove her coat. Maybe this was his way of paying her back for what she had done to him. Maybe he was going to make her realize how powerless she was to resist him, and then he would crush her with one powerful blow as he rejected her.

"Why don't you just tell me how much you hate me, Doug? Why do you have to do it this way!" Her voice shook, a testament that she was about to lose control of her tightly clenched emotions.

"What! Hate you!" Doug threw her coat onto a chair and turned back to face her, his puzzlement taking the place of desire. "I don't hate you, Katherine. Why on earth would I?"

"Because of what I did to you." She was so confused, and the tears began to well up in her eyes, making everything out of focus. "I almost ruined your career!"

"Katherine." Doug grasped both of her shoulders, forcing her to look at him. "I almost lost something much more important to me than my career." His blue eyes traveled across her face, memorizing each feature again, ingraining them even further upon his mind. "Tell me I didn't lose it, Katherine."

What did he want her to say! She didn't understand him. Surely he wasn't referring to her, to their relationship! And if so, which relationship? "I'm not sure I know what you mean, Doug."

"Our relationship, what we had between us!" He seemed genuinely perplexed that she didn't understand what he meant. "We had—have—something very special,

Katherine. Something stronger than all our past difficulties and misunderstandings."

"We had a good sexual relationship, that's true." She tried to avoid looking directly at him. But it was difficult. He was so close, his chest so near. All she had to do was lift her hands and she could run them across the wide expanse of his shirt . . . unfasten the buttons . . . touch his skin . . . God, she had to think about something else!

"Sex? Is that all we had between us?" Doug stepped back as if stung, removing his body from her fantasy. Shoving his hands into the back pockets of his slacks, he began pacing, resembling once again that caged animal she had seen in him before.

"Katherine, I have thought of little else but you since I first met you three years ago. Sure, sex was a part of it. I'd be lying through my teeth if I said I didn't think about making love to you. I dream of it and think of it constantly." He stopped and raked his hand through his hair with agitation. "But it was more than that. It was you that I fell in love with. The woman who tried constantly to crawl under my skin at every press conference, the one who made all my success come alive for me. I thought it was more than sex for you too, Kathe—"

"I love you, Doug." For a minute he was silent, not sure if he had heard her correctly or not. When he looked at her, he knew. It was in her eyes, overshadowing all the doubts and all the hurt. It shone like emeralds in her eyes. "I've always loved you, since I first met you in Springfield. I loved you and—and I hated you because I thought I could never have you."

"Katherine . . ." He sighed her name in a mixture of relief and deep affection as he walked back to her and enfolded her in his strong embrace.

"But I want more than that, Doug."

"More than love?" He pulled his head back to study her face.

"I want to be your friend."

"You are, Katherine. I couldn't think of anyone I'd rather have for a friend than you."

"But—but you said when we were near the car that it was too late for us to be friends." It was still so confusing, so incomplete in her mind. She wanted Doug in every sense of the word, and she wanted him to feel the same way.

Doug frowned as he thought back to the conversation. Finally he smiled as he remembered. "You said you wanted us to be *just* friends, and I said it was too late for that. We're friends, yes. But, we're more, much more, than just friends."

Kat smiled, too. Sheepishly. How could she have been so stupid? She had protected herself so well, she had been hidden from the words that were actually said between them.

Reaching her hand up, she pressed her palm against his cheek. Her eyes took on a sad glow as she let her fingers glide into his hair. "I'm still so sorry about what I did to you . . . to your reputation. I never believed it. But, I—"

"Katherine." His arms slid around her waist, pulling her up tight against his body. "You did what you had to do. I probably would have done the same thing in your place. We were both at fault, because we didn't communicate with each other. If we committed a wrong, it was that—not being honest with each other about our feelings and our doubts."

"What about Elizabeth? How is she taking it?"

"Elizabeth's still got her law practice. She's a survivor. She'll do just fine."

The huge lump of pent-up emotions that were blocking Kat's throat prevented her from speaking, but she lifted her other hand to Doug's cheek and pulled his face toward hers. It was just as well she couldn't talk. This was what she wanted to do anyway.

She touched her lips gently to his, letting him mold them to his own. When his mouth closed over hers, she felt all the love of the past three years pouring out of her and into him. Her arms wrapped tightly around his neck while his hands arched her hips into the thrust of his. She strained toward him, wanting to be absorbed by his strength, by his desire.

His mouth pulled away from her parted lips, and his tongue grazed a slow path to her ear, tasting and devouring every inch of flesh as it moved. "What would you think of being married to an old golf bum?" His mouth dropped to her neck. He wanted her answer, and wanted her to know how much he wanted her with him always, but his physical needs for her were so great. He wanted to make love to her first. They could talk later. Much later.

She tilted back her head to meet his mouth and tongue, wanting to answer him and let him know the thrill that passed through her when she thought of being his wife. But just then the thrill of his tongue on her shoulder, where he had pulled her blouse aside, was so heavenly. . . . "I think"—her hands slipped down from behind his neck and began slowly unfastening the buttons of his shirt —"I think I would marry you even if—" She kissed his hair-covered chest where the shirt was now open. She could feel his heart pounding under the surface and heard the low, rumbling groan inside him as her tongue moved across it to entice one hair-encircled nipple. "God, yes, I'll marry you!" Their mouths collided, the answer already evident to both of them anyway.

His tongue roamed the inside of her mouth with an urgency that left them both weak. His hand moved to the front of her blouse, opening it, lifting her bra and pulling her naked breasts against his hard bare chest. His hair against her nipples made the already over-sensitized nerve endings tingle, but she pressed herself tighter against him, trying to crawl inside him.

His hand moved between them once again to release the snap and zipper of her corduroy jeans. "God, if you only knew how badly I've wanted you, Katherine. Every time I saw you, I wanted to throw you to the ground and love you until you had no strength to resist me." His warm words against her mouth stoked the fire within her, and her fingernails raked a long, slow trail down his bare back.

His hands slipped inside the back of her jeans and then her panties, his fingers pressing into the naked skin of her hips, pulling her into the hardened muscle between his thighs.

"I guess—" Kat's breath was ragged and heavy, the tightening in her lower stomach almost too much to control. "I suppose we are—sex—ually—compat—pat ible—" Her laugh never made it to her throat, the sighs of her desire taking its place.

She hadn't expected an answer, but then she hadn't expected his almost painful reaction either. He groaned, an animalistic sound that encompassed all the deep-seated pain and need and love and hunger. His fingers plunged between her thighs from behind, the warmth and moistness waiting for his deep, caressing exploration. Her hips began moving, slowly, rhythmically, against him, and all the while his tongue explored her mouth and throat and ears and hair.

She never dreamed it could be like this, this soaring flight that took her higher and higher until she felt she would explode. Her hands were set loose in a torrent of restless wanderings across his back and jean-clad hips and inner thighs. She pulled her hand around between them, touching him as he was touching her.

But suddenly he pulled back, closed his eyes tightly, and let out a long, slow, tortured breath. Cupping her face in his hands, he spoke in ragged spurts. "Not—yet. I want to love—your body the way it should be loved. I don't—want to get to the point"—he breathed deeply again—"where I have to rush. Do you understand what I'm—trying to—"

She nodded without having a clue as to what he was mumbling about. All she knew was that she didn't want him to stop touching her. Whatever he wanted was just fine. . . .

She leaned her head back as he pushed her shirt and her bra off her arms and moved his mouth slowly across the soft mound of one of her breasts, his tongue circling the nipple time and again. When his mouth closed over it tighter and began to draw it into his mouth, she felt the quickening in her stomach increase, the need climbing to the point where she thought she could stand it no longer. As his mouth moved to her other breast to capture it in the same feverish manner, her arms wrapped around his shoulders, holding him against her so that he would never stop this delicious torture.

He did stop, but the sweet agony of his mouth against her skin did not end there. Lowering himself to his knees, his mouth played across her stomach while his hands pulled her jeans and panties down over her hips and down around her ankles.

She didn't remember stepping out of them. She didn't remember leaning into him. All she was aware of was the burning trail that his tongue blazed across her body, kissing, tasting, exploring, worshiping every square inch until she felt that she would explode unless the fire was extinguished and the hunger assuaged.

"Doug!" Her hands were holding his head, her fingers grasping the strands of his hair. "Please!" At that moment her knees weakened and collapsed. She fell into his waiting arms, where he lifted her and carried her to his bed.

She didn't want to lose him even for the time it took for him to remove his shirt and pants, but he accomplished it in record time, his own raging desires now beyond the slow-moving stage.

As he eased between her waiting thighs their mouths fused together in a sweeping embrace of their love on all of its levels. It was a love that surged beyond the physical, lifting them above all the misunderstandings and imperfections. It was a love that would hold them together always.

Afterward Doug lay on his back with Kat's head resting on his chest. Her breathing was still uneven, and she could feel the rapid beating of his heart beneath her cheek.

"Doug, I never knew it could be like that. I guess I have a lot to learn." She kissed his chest, her fingers gliding through the brown hair curled tightly against his skin.

"That's what I like, a willing pupil." He ran his hand up and down her spine, letting it rest gently on her hipbone.

"I love you, you know that, don't you?"

"Yes." She knew.

"And nothing will come between us ever again."

"No, never."

"Our careers will never be more important than our marriage."

"Nothing will. But I'm not writing anymore, Doug. I gave it up."

"Why? No, don't answer that. I think I know why. But I also know you'll go back to it."

"I really don't care about that anymore, Doug. All I want—"

"I know." He pressed her hip hard against his thigh, his other hand tunneling under the mass of her red hair. "Right now, you think that this is all you could ever want. But later, you'll miss your writing. You'll miss following the Tour. You're good at it, Katherine, and I know how much you love it. I could always tell that, even when I found it hard to accept gracefully your criticism of me."

"Well, I can tell you one skill about which you will certainly never get criticism from me." She laughed seductively, and her tongue raked across his chest.

He rolled over on top of her, pinning her beneath his long, lean frame. "Oh, yeah? You mean when it comes to rolling in the hay, I take the lead?"

"Most definitely."

"Good. And, I do hope that when you start writing again, you won't dwell so much on my swinging."

"No," she purred. "You won't have time to do much swinging with me around. No, I think I'll concentrate instead on your powerful stroke."

"Hey." He laughed, pressing her down into the mattress with his weight. "Are you sure your editors won't have to mail your articles in plain brown wrappers?" He was nuzzling her neck with his mouth, and her own hands grasped at the firm muscles of his hips. As his hand moved under her hips and between her thighs once more, Kat sighed with the longing that she was feeling again and knew she would always feel with this man.

But without warning he removed his hand from her body and sat up on the bed, an expression of affected sobriety in his posture and face.

Kat opened her eyes in stunned surprise. "Is something the matter?" She frowned and sat up beside him.

He smiled wickedly. "Well, earlier you expressed your desire for more than the physical side of our relationship, so . . ." He paused and draped the blanket primly over his thighs, laughter sprinting across the surface of his eyes. "I thought maybe we should work on the friendship part. You did want to be friends, didn't you?" he asked with mock-seriousness.

Kat rose quickly to her knees and in one swift shove pushed Doug back against the mattress. Climbing on top of him, she held his hands behind his head. Lowering her mouth to his, she smiled mischievously. "Let's just take our relationship one step at a time, shall we?"

When his mouth rose up to meet hers and his hands broke from their bondage to clasp her to him, she knew he couldn't have agreed more.

LOOK FOR NEXT MONTH'S
CANDLELIGHT ECSTASY ROMANCES™:

78 A FATAL ATTRACTION, *Shirley Hart*
79 POWER PLAY, *Jayne Castle*
80 RELENTLESS LOVE, *Hayton Monteith*
81 BY LOVE BETRAYED, *Anne N. Reisser*
82 TO CATCH THE WILD WIND, *Jo Calloway*
83 A FIRE OF THE SOUL, *Ginger Chambers*